UNTAMED FORCE

Force of Nature Series
Book 4

By

KATHI S. BARTON

World Castle Publishing

KATHI S. BARTON

WCP
World Castle Publishing
Pensacola, Florida

Copyright © Kathi S. Barton 2013
ISBN: 9781938961885
First Edition World Castle Publishing February 4, 2013
http://www.worldcastlepublishing.com

Cover: Karen Fuller
Photos: Shutterstock
Editor: Brieanna Robertson

CHAPTER 1

He was suddenly awake. He felt his wolf start to take him when a whispered voice near his ear spoke. He couldn't see her in the darkness as she'd put her hands over his mouth and eyes.

"Rein him in or he will pull mine. And calm your eyes. We've enough to do without a couple of snarling wolves to add to it. Pull him, Dallas, or I will be forced to leave."

He tried. But his wolf wanted to smell the woman next to his bed, wanted to taste her scent, but even flaring his nostrils could not bring her to him. His wolf, however, didn't care. He wanted her now. He wanted Dallas to pull her into his bed and bite her, fuck her until she was his, mate with her. Her low growl told him he wasn't doing as she'd asked, but was making it harder. He was harder too.

"Dallas, I will hurt you if you do not stop that. I cannot think when you smell like that to me." She was suddenly gone and he lay on his bed with her warmth still tingling over his mouth and eyes.

"Come back here," he said, his voice low and hard. His wolf. He was telling her to come to them. "Now, Stacy. Come here."

She hesitated for a minute. He could feel her struggle and he wanted her to lose. Moving to the edge of the bed, he started to rise when he heard a child cry out from the other room. He looked at her sharply as she moved into the hall.

"There's been a killing. A wolf from another pack. His family is down in the kitchen seeking shelter for fear of their pack alpha. The dead wolf's mate is downstairs with her family. The alpha is going to kill them because, he claims, he was hurt when her mate did not protect him."

"How was he hurt? Badly?" Stacy shook her head. "Then why does he want to kill the family?"

"Because the man died too quickly when he murdered him and he feels that he did not get his reward." She looked down the hall toward where his kitchen was. "The woman has been hurt. One of the cubs is…I have called for the doctor. I don't know if he will make it."

"Call Phil. Have him or Holly come. They can sometimes help when it's close." He stood, not caring that she could see him naked. His cock was still straining from his body. "Next time you come to my room, it won't be for conversation."

She nodded. "Then I will send in another. I was wrong to invade your bedroom. But I did not want you to come to us with…please dress. They await you."

Suddenly, she was gone. Dallas looked down at his cock and tried to will it to relax. The woman was driving him nuts and he didn't know what to do about it. Then there was the added fact that she was living with another male. Christ, he didn't know why this woman, of all females in their growing pack, affected him like this. Going to his bathroom he turned the water to cold and stepped in. Even his wolf snarling at him couldn't bring him down. Reaching for his cock, he did the only thing he could think to do.

Thinking about her over him, he closed his eyes as he stroked his cock. He'd never seen her naked. Even during pack meetings she was careful to stay away from them all. But he'd seen her clothed and knew that she'd be lovely.

It only took seconds for him to come; spraying his cum along the tile wasn't even close to being satisfying. But it did take the edge off. For now. Soon, he tried to tell his body and his wolf. Very soon, he'd find a female and fuck her until he could sleep at night without waking in a cold sweat and a hard-on.

There were nine people in his kitchen when he walked in. Phil had come and Holly was with him. His sister was holding one of the smaller cubs. Phil had his back to the family with his wrist over the tiny mouth of the bloodied babe. When he looked at Dallas, Phil smiled. He'd been able to save it.

"He will punish you if he knows where we are. He said that no place would be far enough for us to hide." Dallas looked at the woman and sat down. She cowered away from him. "Please don't hit me too. I've got to care for my young."

"I never hit a woman. My brother is alpha here and he'll make sure you're safe." He looked at Stacy. "Have you called Austin?"

"He did not answer. I have sent one of the others milling about out of doors to his home. Can you contact him?"

Dallas nodded. He should have thought of that.

"Take the little ones downstairs and—"

"No. No, please don't take them from me. I won't have you kill them when I'm not there. Please, they're all I have."

Dallas felt his anger boil over, but he pulled it in. This woman was terrified and didn't know him.

"There are rooms downstairs. Bedrooms we use when one of the pack or another pack needs shelter. If you'd like to go down and look for yourself, that'll be fine. But they are exhausted and will feel better once they are rested." He nodded to Stacy and Holly. "You've met them, so they'll take them down with you."

"Here is your son, Mrs. Reynolds. He'll be fine. I've put him into a deeper sleep, but as you can see, he's breathing better already." Phil handed over her baby and the woman started to cry more.

"He tossed him across the room as if he was no more than a pillow. I knew he was hurt and we shouldn't have moved him, but the bastard was going for him again. I had to fight back. I had to save my children. He killed my mate." Sobbing now, she leaned against Holly. "I've nowhere to go. He'll kill us all for justice."

Phil cupped the back of the woman's head and held her. She calmed almost immediately, and soon she was asleep. Phil didn't let her go, but picked her up and carried her to the open basement door. When the kitchen was empty Dallas reached for his brother.

"We've a major problem here. I need you to come to the house. I've a family here that needs shelter from their alpha."

"One of your minions just woke my children. He's lucky that CJ didn't kill him. Ever hear of a fucking phone?" There was hardness to his voice, but also a small bit of humor.

"Is it on, moron? I know you have a habit of turning it off when you're with the kids. Could be you forgot to turn it on again?" Dallas loved his brother's family and CJ was by far the most beautiful alpha person he'd ever met. He felt his brother's anger.

"It's off. I'm on my way. What do you know?" He told him nothing other than Phil had saved one of the children from death. *"Make sure there is extra coverage on the grounds. Have Gordon run a check on the alpha when you get me a name."*

Stacy came through the door, sat at the table, and pushed a sheet of paper at him. *"His name is Rich Sterling and the pack is already touring the grounds. Also, you should know that he killed one of his pack members because he was harmed. I'm not sure…I don't have a lot of details on that yet. The woman, I have her in the basement with her five cubs."*

"We're on our way. CJ has called Mom too. We might need some extra food brought in as well." He heard his brother laugh. *"CJ said to tell you not to hurt Stacy. Alexis will kick your ass."*

Dallas looked over at the woman in question and told his brother to fuck off. He tried again to bring her scent into his body, but all he could smell was the family. He wanted to ask her about it, but Phil coming up from the basement made him stop. Later, he'd get his answers and then he'd take her to his bed.

"The family is asleep. I hope you don't mind, but they were terrified and it wasn't going to get any better with their mother screaming that she was afraid." Phil sat at the table as he continued and he pulled Holly onto his lap and held her to him. "Her mate was the man's second, or I think maybe his enforcer. I'm never sure of the terminology, but I'm learning. When the alpha came to her home earlier tonight he told them that he was going to kill them all for an injustice. Is that possible that he could do that?"

Dallas nodded. "If the man was his enforcer then, yes, he could according to pack law. How badly was he hurt? And how did you…you read her mind."

"Yes. I don't know what happened with the alpha and this woman's mate, but the alpha, Lord Sterling, he has them call him, has already killed her brother. And still wanted more. The child I saved was the first he encountered when he broke their front door down and entered their…house. I have to tell you, from what I've seen, it's not much bigger than my shed out back. And the shed is in better shape. If he does that for his employees, then I shudder to think what the rest of his pack lives in."

Austin entered after a short knock. His brother was the alpha of this pack and when he entered a room, it showed. Dallas was his enforcer as well as his twin. And even though Dallas was slightly bigger Austin could and would command his death if need be.

"Gordon is on his way via car. He has my mate and cubs with him. Can they bed down in the upper levels until we figure out what this is concerning? I want to help the family, but I don't want to get caught with our pants down." Dallas nodded and watched as his brother pulled on some jeans he always had here. "Thanks, Phil, for helping out. Is the child going to make it?"

"Yes. There was some internal damage done and without proper care or my blood he would have died. I've put them to sleep to rest. But I was just telling your brother here what happened. You don't have to worry this is a ruse, but I would be careful. This alpha is a nut ball."

Dallas laughed and sobered when Stacy glared at him. The woman was driving him insane. He looked up when the rest of his family came in. His mother was directing some of the younger wolves that were always around to put the food in the pantry. He kissed her cheek and asked what he could do to help.

Austin may be pack alpha, leader of nearly a hundred wolves now, but their mother ruled the roost. Each person in the kitchen knew it too. When she said she needed something every person in the pack would scramble to get it. She was queen as far as they were concerned.

"Get me that skillet. How long will they be down for, Phil?" He told her a couple of hours. "Good. I'll have plenty of time to get some food ready. There are more pack coming, I think. Phil, go and get those extra dishes. Holly, see what you can do about getting the bottled water from the storage unit and, the rest of you, get the tables set up in the yard. I got a feeling it's going to be a long night."

As everyone took off to do her bidding Dallas and Gordon sat at the table and began figuring out what they could find on the man who had interrupted their lives. Stacy sat down, too, after Austin asked her to.

Stacy had not pledged to the pack, but to Alexis, Gordon's mate. Austin could ask her to help, but he couldn't really command her. She was skittish enough as it was. No one but maybe Alexis knew her whole story. All they knew was that she'd been thrown from her pack because they claimed that she was barren. No one knew how that had made her unworthy of pack, but they were glad for her help.

"Tell me how you found them. I'm assuming they weren't on our property when you came across them," Austin asked her. "And what do you know of this alpha?"

"I was...I can tell you all you want to know about him. He was my pack leader." She looked around the room and then dropped her head. "He's also my father."

Dallas felt his wolf stir to protect her. When Stacy looked up at him she growled low. She was the prickliest person he knew. He let a little of his wolf go to show her that he was bigger and badder. She did the same and soon it went from a pissing contest to need.

"Behave, both of you. Damn it all to hell, the two of you act like teenagers in heat. Either fuck it out of your systems or stay away from each other." Austin got up to pace. "Your father? You said your last name is O'Brien. I thought you said his name was Sterling."

"He is. I am…I'm his child because he and my mother were mates before he became pack leader. When she had me, he noticed that…that I wasn't quite right. And not being a son had him turn on me and her. My mother died the night he was given the pack. I never knew what happened, but I think he might have murdered her."

No one spoke. No one asked. Dallas wanted to pull her into his arms and hold her. He looked up at his mom and saw her staring at him. He couldn't tell what she was thinking, so he got up to hold her. She hit him with her ever present wooden spoon.

"What the hell was that for?" She hit him again then walked into the other room. And of course, like a fool, he followed her. "Mom, as soon as you put that thing down I'm going to smash it to splinters. What are you hitting me for?"

"You are not my son if you are that dense." She turned back to the table where the plates and bottled water had been stacked. "Men are…I can't believe your father and I raised such a…do you not know comfort?"

He looked at her then toward the kitchen where Stacy still was. "Her? She'd as soon rip my head off as let me touch her. I've tried."

She turned on him then. And he took several steps back when she lifted the spoon again. "Try harder."

When she left the room he stood there for several minutes. Try harder? Try harder at what? Getting her to tear him up or… Dallas looked back at the kitchen, then at the table where she'd been standing. Was she telling him to take her to his bed? No, that couldn't be right. She had to know the woman hated him. Then he saw the spoon.

Picking it up, he was very tempted to do just what he said he was going to do, but he thought maybe that would get him in more trouble than it was worth. He knew she more than likely had a crate of them somewhere and was tempting him with this one. He put the spoon in his back pocket and went to his office. He had to think and the others had this under control.

~~~

Rich watched the house burn. He'd come back tonight to get the bitch, but found not only the house empty of them, but it seemed that others, wolves he'd not smelled before, had been here too.

He could smell death and smiled that he'd killed the babe. He wasn't going to have another man's cub come for him someday. He had been disappointed that he'd not been able to do more than beat the woman a little, but when a wolf had come out of nowhere and attacked him he'd had to leave. Now he had another second and he was ready for the fucking wolf to come again. Then he'd found the stupid woman gone and her brats as well and he wasn't happy about it.

"There's no trace of them here. It's like someone came back and marked the area so we couldn't find them."

Rich didn't even glance at the man beside him. Moron, he already had figured that out.

"I'm sending pack out to see where she's hiding."

"No, don't. She's not within the…wait. Yes, go ahead. And though you won't find her or any trace of her, make an example of a few of the others you come across simply because we can't find her. Tell them we think she's hiding with them. Tell them we can smell her on them and we know that they're harboring her. Then burn down their homes." He could feel the man hesitate, but he said that he would.

Rich didn't just run a large pack of wolves like he was a leader. He ruled them because they were terrified of him. And none of the families in his pack would run because they knew that he'd hunt them down and kill them. So they stayed. But this bitch hadn't. She'd run and he'd find her and kill her along with her cubs, as well as whoever had her. He looked to the north and wondered if she had gone that way to the little pack in Canada. Rich was going to have her and the rest of them by week's end or else.

He shifted and ran back to his home. He had to bathe to try and get the stench of the hovel he'd just left off him before dinner. He let them have homes; the very least they could do was to keep them clean. He knew there was no electricity. He didn't think it necessary for staying in a house long enough to eat, sleep, and fuck. There were other means of getting hot water when there was none in the house. Build a fucking fire and clean the place up.

He was in the shower when he heard someone in the outer room. Smiling, he waited for her to come to him. He'd left word at the house that he wanted a female and they knew better than to not do as he asked. When he opened the door to the shower she stood there naked.

"Come here," he commanded. She took small steps to get to him so he reached out and yanked her to him. When she fell into the shower, landing on her knees, he shoved his cock in her mouth. "Perfect."

She wasn't very good at blowing him, he discovered, or she just didn't care to service her alpha. Grabbing a handful of her hair he yanked her head up. "Do it or die. It's up to you."

After that she started to do it correctly. And after a few minutes, she began to moan. Rich leaned back against the tile and watched her through hooded eyes. This was what he needed, a good blow job. Pumping into her mouth, she reached between her legs to service herself. He was too far gone to stop her. Normally he didn't allow it, but right now he needed release more than he needed her to behave. When he came with a growl she did as well and he nearly came again when she rammed her finger up his ass.

"Christ," he hissed at her as she swallowed him down the back of her throat, and he fucked her harder. His balls tightened as she moved her finger in and out of him and before he could stop it, he came again.

He couldn't move. He'd not had that kind of orgasm in years. He looked down at the bitch as she sat staring up at him. She had cum on her chin and the look of hunger in her eyes as she eyed his semi-hard cock.

"You want me again?" She nodded. "Go to the bedroom and lay there and wait for me. As soon as I get your smell off me I'm going to fuck your ass until you bleed."

She nodded again and stood. He backhanded her. "I didn't tell you to go yet, did I?"

When he allowed her to leave he finished his shower and got dressed. He would fuck her, but on his terms, not hers. When he went into the bedroom he nearly changed his mind. She was standing next to the bed with her legs wide and her pussy dripping with need. Walking up behind her he slapped her ass and she moaned.

"I want you to be here when I return. Naked and waiting whenever I want to fuck you." He ran his finger through her cream and took it to his mouth. "And when you fail to satisfy me even one time, you'll die."

He left the room and smiled. She'd be there when he returned, he had no doubt. And even if she had to work for hours, he knew that he'd never leave this room without being fully sated. Rich loved his life as an alpha.

KATHI S. BARTON

CHAPTER 2

The mood around the compound made her nervous. It was necessary, but no less nerve-racking. Stacy moved along the fence, trying to avoid all the others, and watched for her mistress. She was supposed to meet her here in half an hour. She heard her coming, shifted to human, and dressed.

"I swear to you it's a real pleasure some days to get out of the studio. Today being one of them." Alexis moved with the grace of a queen and Stacy found herself wanting to try and emulate her. "I came when I got your message. Is it Dallas again?"

"No...yes. But not all. I need you to help me, mistress. There is a man in the pack that should not be here. He is...he is a sadist and has taken to hurting the females." This was not the first time that she had gone to Alexis about a pack member. And probably would not be the last. "He is now, as we speak, with a woman that is not his."

"Tell me where and I'll have Gordon catch him." Stacy told her and she knew when her mistress contacted her mate. "He's on his way now. And not alone this time."

A month ago Gordon had gone where Stacy had told him when something almost as bad was going on. But that time he had gone alone. He had been hurt badly, but the wolf he had gone after had died. Gordon was swift and final in his protection of his brother's pack. It was the only reason she stayed. Well, that and Dallas, the stupid jerk.

"Dallas has said that he wants me. I do not know how to tell him again I am not worthy."

Alexis snorted.

"I am without scent, my lady, and will not be a good mate to him."

"The only person that cares you have no scent is you. Go to him. Let him mate with you. You couldn't find a better man." She paused. "Gordon is at the house. He said he would tell me later what happens. Austin is with him."

This would not end well and she knew it. Austin was a very good alpha, but he demanded respect. Not just to him, but to his pack as well. Anyone caught hitting another without just cause was banned from the pack and, if severe enough, he would kill them. The law had been around for centuries, but few followed it like Austin did.

"Tell me about Dallas. What makes you afraid of him?"

Stacy started to say she was not afraid of anyone, but Alexis continued.

"I know you are afraid of something about him. Tell me what it is, Stacy. The man practically drools when you're in the same room as him."

"He is just in need of release." She flushed when she realized what she had said. "He is a man and has needs. I will not...I do not think I can...I am a woman who has had little experience with men."

"You've had no experience with men except for the kind that beat you. Dallas would rather die than to harm you, or any person for that matter. I don't understand why you don't just speak to him about it."

Because she was terrified he would take her out of pity. She would rather die than have a mate that felt sorry for her.

She looked away when she felt Alexis probe her mind. "It will do you no good, my lady. You have not enough experience to get what you want and I am not giving you what I share with no one. Dallas is a good man and I will not allow him to be shunned because I wanted him to take me. If you would give me permission I would leave your pack and join another."

"You do that and I will hunt you down myself."

Stacy looked at the woman who never even raised her voice to her children, but just had to her.

"I mean it. You leave me and I'll have you hunted down and brought back. What kind of shame do you think you'd do to me? And my children would be hurt too."

Stacy nodded. She loved the children that Alexis had brought to this pack. Even humans, as these were. They made her feel there was some good in the world. And she especially liked the younger boy Jake. He was a thinker and she loved him. "I will not leave, but you will please not bring up Dallas to me again. He is going to find a mate soon and things with him and me will no longer be an issue." She put out her hand to shake on it. Alexis smiled and Stacy thought the woman had something else up her sleeve, but could not think what it would be.

"I will not bring Dallas up to you again. You will not hear another word from me about him unless you bring him up first. Deal?"

They shook, but Stacy thought she had missed something. But Alexis changed the subject.

"They have the man. Austin is taking him to the cells now. There will be a trial on the next moon phase."

Alexis went back to her studio to make more of her pretty things for her shop. She envied the woman and her talent. Stacy could fight well and could do anything a man could do, but she could not be a girly girl. Alexis had been kind to her and she thought it was not because she felt sorry for her either. But Stacy still felt the best course of action was to leave. She shifted to wolf and followed her mistress just far enough back so as not to alarm her. Alexis thought no one would come after her and Stacy made sure no one did.

She thought about Dallas when she saw her mistress enter the building. He was a beautiful man. She wondered briefly if men were beautiful and decided it did not matter. To her, he was. His hair was dark as night and his eyes made her think things about him she had never thought before about a man. Things like his eyes looked like the summer sky. His skin, dark from working outdoors, made her want to touch him, run her fingers over him, and taste at him.

When she had been in his bedroom that morning, she had been tempted to crawl into bed with him. But she had not because, beyond that, she did not think she could please him. He would expect a woman in his bed to pleasure him and not be a novice like her. But her breasts still prickled when she thought of his voice this morn. Full of lust and need. It made her want to find him now and have him take her.

When he appeared in front of her suddenly she thought she had called to him. But he had not seen her as yet, so she pressed low into the earth and stilled herself. He was stomping around the dirt and muttering to himself. He was saying things that made no sense to her, but she stayed where she was. Now would not be a good time for him to find her.

When he stopped suddenly she felt the hair on her back rise. He'd seen her. "Show yourself or I'll attack. I'm in the mood to have a go at just about anyone."

She didn't shift, but stood. He looked at her for a long time and she felt her hackles rise. If he wanted to fight she was probably in the same frame of mind to take him on. When he started to strip down to his skin, she nearly bolted.

"You leave and I'll chase you down. If you want to spar with me, I'll have you know that I'm not going to go easy on you because you're a female."

She growled low, letting him know that she did not think he could best her anyway. When he was standing before her naked she tried her best not to stare at his hard cock.

"We could spend our energy another way if you'd come to me in human form. Right now, the thought of burying myself into your heat has me seeing stars."

She was glad she was wolf and that he could not see her blush.

"What's it going to be Stacy?"

She lunged at him and thought to catch him off guard. She should have known better. He was an enforcer and prepared at all times to be attacked. His shift was quick and fluid. He was a human male one second and snarling wolf the next. She attacked again, showing him she was not afraid.

~~~

Dallas didn't think she'd go for sex over fighting. But one could hope, he supposed. He wanted her so badly right now that he almost wanted to command her to shift so that he could have her. She was keeping him up at night, or at least thoughts of her were keeping him up at night.

When she lunged at him he nearly forgot to shift; she was so beautiful in motion. But he had shifted and was glad for it because it seemed she wasn't holding back either. Her canines nearly missed his throat. The second attack had him thinking this was going to be fun. But when she came at him again he thought he might be in trouble.

He would never hurt her, no matter what he said to her. She was a female and much smaller than him. But she had been trained to fight and she was fucking good at it. When he pinned her twice in a row he nearly let her up, but he decided that he'd had enough fighting and wanted her just where he had her. He shifted, holding down her wolf for several seconds to see if she would as well.

"Shift. Now, Stacy." She whimpered and tried to get away, but he held her down. "Shift." He'd put as little command in his voice as he could, wanting her to shift because she wanted, not because he'd commanded her to. When her fur started to recede, he held himself off her slightly, but didn't let her go.

"You cannot make me have sex with you."

He was reasonably sure he could, but said nothing to the furious woman beneath him.

"Get off me Dallas. I am not your female."

"You could be."

She shook her head.

"I want you. I want to make love to you right now, Stacy, but I won't take you against your will." He nuzzled her throat and licked along her pounding pulse. "I want to taste you. Lick you over your entire body until you beg me to take you."

"No. You cannot."

He moved down to her hard nipple and licked it before taking it into his mouth and sucking.

"Please do not do this. You should be with someone else if you only wish to ease your need."

He rocked into her soft folds and felt her wetness. He looked down at her again as he rocked harder. "You're wet for me. Let me show you how much wetter I can make you. Or let me eat your pussy until you come. I want to taste you when you come down my throat." She moaned when he rocked this time and he thought that he had won, but then he saw the tears in her eyes and he couldn't do it. He rolled off her and onto his back.

He heard her roll away from him, but he didn't look. He was afraid if he saw her nakedness, he'd forget that he was a gentleman and take her anyway. His cock ached for release and he didn't think he'd ever be able to jerk off enough to ease this one.

"I can send another female to you if you'd like. I am sure there are many that would ease—"

"Don't. Just go please and leave me to myself." He closed his eyes and thought of her taste on his tongue. "You're the one I want and no other will do." He looked at her when he felt her shift. "You and I aren't finished, Stacy. You will have to either tell me a good reason I can't have you or I will do just that. Something is between us and you feel it too."

She took off through the woods without a sound. Dallas laid there for several more minutes before he felt if he stood up his cock wouldn't hurt him. He laughed when he pulled on his pants. If this kept up, he was going to have to have himself neutered just to be around her. He doubt that would help.

He pulled on his boots and headed to the pack house. He wasn't going to be fit to be around anyone for the rest of the day so he might go see if he could get Connor to fight with him. Probably. He was always up for a good run if not.

The woman, Georgia Reynolds, had awakened around six this morning. She'd been in his kitchen with his mom when he'd come down after going up to shower again. He'd been trying to help Alexis with a heavy crate to take to the shop when one of the bottles of bath oil had broken. She'd laughed at him for twenty minutes before he told her he'd send someone else to help. She was still laughing as he left her.

Women. He neither understood them nor did he figure he ever would.

"She said that she has to do something to help out. I let her feed the children." His mom shook her head when he started to ask why that would have been a problem.

"I've not had the pleasure of electric for some time, master. It is a great deal easier to cook when you've no need to build a fire."

Dallas looked at his mom when Georgia said that.

"They aren't allowed any luxuries at the other place because it is an unnecessary financial drain on the pack. She said only the alpha has running water and heat. He is allowed this because he cares for them." His mom looked at the woman before she continued. "They don't get paid for working either. If they grow a garden or have fruit trees on their property they owe half of it to the pack and the alpha uses the money he gets from selling it as support to the pack as a whole."

Dallas had a thousand questions run through his head. Most of which had to do with how to find this bastard. He tried to find a way to gently ask something while he tried to control his beast. "And when he killed your mate, did he give you a reason for that? I mean, how badly was he hurt that he felt justified the death of a family?" Dallas watched the woman stiffen then his mom pulled her to the table.

"Georgia, I swear to you, you're safe here. Austin is a good pack leader and he'll keep you safe. And he would never treat anyone as it looks like you've been treated."

She took a tissue from his mom before she spoke. "My mate, Tim, hadn't been his enforcer for long. They just don't last long in that position with our alpha. And he'd been afraid from the beginning. When he and the others had gone with the alpha on a hunt Tim had told me to hide until he returned and if he didn't, I was to run with the children. We were packing up to do so when Lord Sterling returned." She took the tissue and began to tear it into shreds. "We'd been in this pack for some years, but never…it was forbidden to leave, you see. He said…he would hunt the runners down and bring them back. I only saw it happen once. He would tie them to the ground and…" She stood then and went to the sink. "My sister and her family knew that things weren't right there and decided they'd had enough. We all thought the same thing, but we had nowhere to go. When he tied them to the ground and then set fire to them I thought I would die. I can still hear their screams in my dreams."

Dallas had to clear his throat twice before he could speak. His mom was crying softly beside him. "Children? Were there any children that he burned?"

Georgia nodded. "Four little ones. Two under the age of five, the other two just nine and ten. If I go back, or he finds me, he'll do worse to mine. He was extremely angry that Tim had allowed him to be hurt."

Dallas had to leave. He had wanted to hunt the man down himself and stake him to the ground and set fire to his nuts first then work his way around other body parts. But he couldn't. First, it would bring the pack down on his brothers and, if he didn't win, the man…no, he was an animal, would know where Georgia and her family were.

Then he'd run into Stacy. And he'd fucked that up too. Christ, could he not get a break? He came to the pack house just as Austin was going at it with another male in the yard. Both men were bloodied and Dallas wanted more than ever to join in. And from the looks of it the other man wasn't going to be walking for some time. *Good,* Dallas thought.

He knew what kind of man he was and Dallas stood to watch, hoping that some of his own anger would be satisfied by proxy. Watching Austin beat the shit out of the slimy bastard was fun, but he also wanted to make sure the guy didn't get the upper hand. Not that he had much of a chance from the looks of things.

Austin stepped back when the other man didn't rise. Dallas was sure that he wanted to finish the man off, but by law he couldn't. He loved his brother very much, but there were times, like now, that he wished he would bend the rules a bit.

"He nearly killed another man's mate."

Dallas looked over at his brother Gordon when he stepped up beside him.

"Alexis heard about it from Stacy and sent us over to catch him. We were nearly too late. The doctor is looking after her now."

"What was he going to do with another male's mate? Or was simply beating her what he had in mind?"

Gordon shook his head.

"He went there to rape her?"

"Seems so. He didn't expect her to be able to fight back. I guess this isn't the first woman he's tried this on. Only this one was ready for him." Gordon laughed as he continued. "She took a hot poker to his ass. If he'd caught her in the house she said she would have shot his sorry ass, but she'd been out burning brush from some of the clearing they'd been doing."

They watched as the man crawled away finally, begging Austin for forgiveness. There was none, of course, and the man was given two hours to get his crap gathered and get out of the territory. Dallas hoped he didn't make it.

"I think he's finished with his lesson," Dallas said as they all, including Austin, walked toward the house. "Do you think it's possible I can sit down with you two later? I have something more to add about the pack leader. I've had a conversation with Georgia. It seems this other pack leader is a bit of a sadist, more so than the one you just knocked the shit out of. And even more so than we'd first thought."

"Like what? Does he try to rape innocent women in their own homes? Does he blame them for what he considers simply a fuck and nothing more?" Dallas looked toward where the man had gone and Austin patted him on the back. "You can have him if he returns. I've had my fill of the prick. What does this other leader, Sterling, do that so much worse than nearly killing a babe?"

Dallas looked at his brother as they entered the house. "Nothing. Not really. But he doesn't allow them any luxuries such as heat and electricity. But he has them. I'm not even sure they have running water."

Austin shook his head and cursed for several second. He shook his head as if to clear it before answering. His brother didn't have a short fuse, but today had tested him. "Sure. I've a bit to add myself. And I think bastard is a tame word, don't you?" Austin picked up his jacket and tossed it to Gordon as he looked at Dallas. "You can help me take this prick to the other side of the grounds. And just so you know, you smell like female. Might want to get that off you before Stacy smells her on you." Gordon started to walk away, but Dallas called him back.

"You can smell Stacy on me?" He flushed when Austin looked at him hard. "Nothing happened, but…you can scent her?"

"No. Just female, but nothing more. By the way, you might what to talk to Alexis. She told me if I saw you I was to tell you to find her. Something about promises she made and how she needs to talk to you."

KATHI S. BARTON

CHAPTER 3

Rich kicked out at the man curled in a ball at his feet. Fucking bastard wasn't worth even learning his name. And now he was dead. It was getting harder and harder to keep an enforcer to help him out. He knew that he was scraping the bottom of the barrel and was getting men who were more terrified of him than wanted to keep him safe. He walked over to his phone and picked it up.

"Find someone that can replace the idiot I just killed. And if he isn't any better than this one, you'll have the job." He hung up, knowing that his butler would do it at all costs. They knew the life expectancy of an enforcer was small and no one wanted the job.

He moved to the fireplace and leaned against the mantle. He'd not been able to find that fucking bitch either. Rich knew that they all were talking about him and his lack of ability to keep his bitches in line. He snarled at the dead man on the floor and wished he could have another go at him. But dead men were not nearly as much fun as living, whimpering ones. He kicked at the wood near his feet. The door opening behind him had him stiffen, but he knew if anyone tried to kill him, they'd be as dead as the man on the floor.

"I've come to clean up the mess, Lord Sterling."

He wanted to laugh but only nodded.

"Shall I dispose of him as the others?"

"I could care less if you took him home with you to fertilize your garden. Just get him the fuck out of here." Rich had a moment of panic when he realized that the butler knew where all the bodies were, but let it go. Your own brother didn't turn you in to the council no matter what you did. "Harvey, you know what will happen to you if anyone starts asking questions about any of this."

Harvey nodded, but didn't speak. He picked up the dead man and walked out of the room. There wasn't a lot he could do to his brother any more. He had no mate, no children, and their mother had been killed long ago. Harvey didn't have anything thanks to him. He moved to the desk again and tried to think if there was one person in the pack he could bring in.

Over the years the pack numbers had dwindled. He had started out with over a thousand and now he thought he had less than half that, though he wasn't all that sure. He knew that word had gotten around that it wasn't going to be long for this pack, so Rich had made laws to increase the number of members. He'd decreed that every female would have a litter a year without fail of he'd kill her and find one that would. It mattered little to him if they had mates or not. If they didn't have a cub then he'd simply kill them. So far, the numbers seem to be increasing, but not at a rate that he'd hoped for. When his phone rang, he nearly didn't pick it up.

"Rich Sterling, this is Councilman Nigel Briggs. I've heard you've had some problems in your pack."

Rich wanted to snarl at the man to mind his own business.

"I've called to see if the rumors are true."

"Well, since I don't have a clue what you're referring to, I'm not sure how I should answer that." He wondered if that bitch Georgia had contacted them and was sure of it when he spoke next.

"Well, let me see…I have a report that you have invoked the rule of death to your enforcer. I'm not sure we've used that rule in…well, centuries. What sort of harm has befallen you from the neglect of your man?"

Rich closed his eyes and counted to ten. If he told the old bastard what had really happened, he'd be brought before the courts. He doubted very much he'd live long if he told them that his pant leg had gotten muddied when they'd been walking to his car. It really hadn't been the man's fault. It had been completely Rich's, but someone had snickered and his enforcer had been the closest.

"My enforcer…oh you mean Reynolds. Well, it seems that he coveted my female. He has his own wife, you see, and when he started making advances to my bitch, I had to put him down." Rich rolled his eyes. Like he had a bitch at all. "I can't have that sort of thing going on, especially when it involves a man who is supposed to enforce the rules, not use them for his own personal gain."

"I see. Entirely different story than the one I got. I can see where that would…I had no idea you'd taken a mate. Congratulations. Best thing in the world for an alpha to take a mate and breed more of his own. Your numbers have been going down of late and, well, we feel that we may have to come and see what is going on."

Over his dead body, he thought. "Nothing the matter. Just the economy. You know how hard it is for a pack to keep together now days. Younger breeds wanting to strike out on their own and all."

"Yes, but you see, your numbers aren't coming up at all. Not even your births have been reported in the black for some time now." Rich heard him rattling around papers as he continued. "There hasn't been a recordable birth in your pack for a number of years. Oh, there has been a few, ten, over the past five years, but your infant death rate is nearly double that. What could be the problem?"

"I'll have to see who isn't giving you the correct numbers and get back to you on that. I'm sure it's been a great deal more than that." Or it would be soon enough. "I know that there are a number of bitches ready to whelp, but as of...let me get back to you soon." He leaned back in his chair. "I don't suppose you know where Reynolds's mate and family have gone, do you? I can't tell you how concerned I am about them and her children. She must be terrified out of her mind right now."

"No doubt, no doubt. But I only have a missive from another pack leader. I don't recall his name right now, but when you call me with those corrected numbers tomorrow, I'll see if I can locate it."

Rich wasn't happy with the way the call ended, but the stupid bastard on the other end didn't know anything about his pack member and that's all that Rich cared about. He began to pace the room and thought about what he had learned from the call.

So, she was with another pack. Well, that didn't really narrow it down, but it did tell him that he'd have more members by the time he got her back. And get her back he would, along with the pack of the man who dared hide her away from him.

He stopped pacing and moved toward the door where there was a file cabinet. He pulled open two drawers before he found what he'd been looking for. Pulling out the directory he tried to figure out whose territory was close enough to his that she would have been able to get to quickly. There were two that he could get to in a day, one that was further out, and one that was brand new. He dismissed the one that was new. That alpha would be too set on following rules because he would want to make a good impression right now. The council was breathing down everyone's neck and the new guy would want to be on his best behavior.

The one that was out about three hundred miles he marked off too. She had a shit ton of kids and going that far on foot with as badly as he'd beaten her and her brats, she'd have to be local. He picked up his phone and thought about what he was going to do to the pack leader harboring what was his.

"I want the car ready in an hour. And as many of the pack as you can assemble to go and find my bitch." Harvey said he would. "Oh, and by the way, you're coming too."

He didn't know why he wanted his brother there, but decided if he didn't come back, so be it. He was a good butler, but not worth much else. He leaned back in his chair and thought about the pack he was going to destroy. Yes, Alpha Alan Wilkinson wouldn't be doing something so stupid like this again.

Laughing, he wondered if the man had any breedable bitches he could steal off while he was there. This was turning out to be much more fun that he'd thought it would ever be.

~~~

Connor looked around at the destruction that had once been someone's home. He'd snuck onto the property with Phil's help late last night and had come out now to see what they could see. He pulled out his phone and started taking pictures of what once was nothing more than a few slabs of wood surrounding what looked like three two-by-fours. He looked over at Phil who'd just come from the woods behind the house.

"I can't find anything that resembles a house anywhere. She was right. They all seem to live like this. How can he do that to his pack?"

Connor shrugged.

"I can't understand any of this."

"He apparently wanted to keep them beholden to him. And from what Georgia said, they all gave more than they could afford and then some." He took a few more pictures before turning to his brother-in-law. "Will I want to puke again if you take me to where the lord lives?"

"Nah. You should be okay this time." Phil laughed. "Never seen a wolf puke as much as you did. Not even Holly throws up that much." He seemed to forget what he was saying for a minute and Connor nearly leapt at the man.

"She's whelping? Are you insane? What if she...why aren't you taking care of her right this minute?" Connor flushed when Phil laughed. "She's my baby sister and I don't want to think of her having sex with anyone much less having cubs. Especially with a prick like you."

"She didn't have sex with me, Connor, she got pregnant by thought. You moron. I suppose you think your brothers aren't having sex either."

Connor grinned. "They can have all the sex they want. And do, I would imagine. But Holly? She's still just a kid." Connor knew his logic was askew, but he didn't back down. "Especially with a blood-sucking ass like you."

Before they could get to the obvious end to their kidding around they heard something and Phil grabbed him and pulled the shadows around them again. Both men stood as still as the trees around them.

The man who walked toward them looked as battered as Georgia did. Connor watched the man search through the rubble as if he was looking for something. Connor wasn't sure what he'd hoped to find, but the man seemed intent on something. When he pulled a chest from the floor, he thought the man had found a stash of money, but all that he pulled from the small chest was a few canned goods and a package of what looked like moldy bread. But if the look on the man's face was any indication, it might as well have been gold.

After he left, Phil stepped back. "This is horrible. If your brother treated his pack this way, I'd drain him then lay him out in the sun until he burnt to a crisp."

Connor knew just what he meant.

"Are you ready? I can't be here any longer."

Connor nodded and was soon going across the compound at a dizzying speed. He didn't get ill this time, but he did feel his legs tremble a little bit. He didn't ask for help, but Phil led him to a tree and helped him sit.

"Sorry. I didn't slow down when I knew it made you sick. I needed to…I don't know how you stood there with the stench so bad."

Connor raised his hand to say he was fine. "No problem. It was getting to me as well. Let me send these to Austin and Dallas and we'll have a look around the alpha's house. I'm ready to call in the council and have his ass put into chains."

They walked to the house after the pictures uploaded. And Christ, what a house it was. The thing was three stories of brick and wood that made even the rich and famous look poor and unknown. Connor walked around the house twice and still couldn't believe what he was seeing.

"This borders on sickening. I mean, really? Why does he need to wipe their faces in the fact that they are paying him to look this good? I bet you there are Italian suits in every closet too." Phil walked up to the front door. "I'm going to drain the prick and piss on his shoes."

Connor thought he was going to have to knock Phil on his ass to keep him from knocking. Which would have been a good thing but for the car that was coming up the drive. Phil grabbed him from behind again and they stood still on the steps when a man got out of the back of a limo. This had to be the alpha.

"I don't care. Find the bitch and bring her and her filthy brats to me now." It was then that they noticed the device in his ear. He was on a cell phone. "You either bring her to me by the end of the week or you'll be joining your family in the grave out back."

The driver walked around the car after closing the door after the alpha got out and stood there for several minutes. Connor thought the man was looking at them, but Phil spoke to him through their link that they'd established before coming here.

"He can't see us. I think he's watching the alpha or waiting. He might have to wait to be dismissed. If dumb fuck goes in the house without the driver leaving, I'll go and touch him after securing you. All right?"

"Christ, be careful."

The front door to the house slammed shut and the man stood still where he'd been left. Phil moved them both, slower this time, to the edge of the tree line and left him there. Connor didn't have long to wait, maybe ten minutes before he came back. Phil looked ready to explode. "Let's go."

Connor didn't ask what he'd found out. He let Phil wrap his arms around his waist and they were off again. He'd thought they were going back to their pack house, but they were deep in the forest now.

"Phil? Where are we?" The smell of death was strong. And some of it wasn't very old. Phil walked to the large backhoe and then pointed to the hole beside it. Connor was almost afraid to walk to it.

It was about ten feet deep and nearly half filled with bodies. Not only adults, although that was bad enough, but children as well. And not all of them looked as if they'd been there all that long.

"The driver is the alpha's brother. He's to bring the dead out here and drop them in the hole when they're murdered. The brother feels he has nothing left and only helps his brother because he provides him with drugs to forget." Phil's voice was soft, but Connor could hear him. "Sterling killed his mate some years ago because she wouldn't submit to him. So he raped her and then killed her. As punishment to his brother for mating with a cold bitch he'd made him bury her and their unborn child."

"And the others? Surely they all weren't killed by the same man."

Phil shook his head.

"Then what killed them? Who did this?"

"Mostly starvation. Some suicide. Harvey, the brother, makes the rounds once or twice a week to gather them up. He doesn't think he can take it much longer. There are a few there that…they aren't all from this pack. This morning, Sterling attacked a pack of fifty looking for Georgia and her cubs."

Connor took pictures. He couldn't send these, afraid that someone else, CJ or Alexis, would see them. He put his phone away and moved to Phil. He was making a decision that he thought would get his ass chewed out by his brother, but he needed something, anything to take before the board.

"Snatch the brother, the driver. Take him to one of your hidey holes, something that has a steel lining. We need someone to confirm this. Also…Christ, I can't believe I'm asking you this, please don't let Holly see this. I'm begging you. I know she's seen a lot of death, but this...please?"

Keeping secrets between mates was forbidden. But Phil, as a very powerful vamp, was able to do things that no other could. He didn't hesitate to ask him to do this because he loved his sister and didn't want something like this, something so heinous, to spoil her pregnancy. Phil looked ready to say no, but then seemed to change his mind. Connor was suddenly very afraid he'd done something equally as stupid to have Phil keep quiet.

"I'll do it, but you owe me. I need something from you that I...it's about Dallas. Stacy is his mate, but she isn't going to allow him to mate with her. She finds herself to be unworthy. I want you to make him so jealous that he takes her."

Connor agreed. He knew that she loved his brother and knew that he was going through some very rough times trying to figure out what was happening. He knew from Alexis that Stacy wasn't having a very easy time of it either. He wanted them both to be happy.

Connor sat as far away from the pit as he could after Phil left. He knew he'd only be gone a few minutes, but it seemed an eternity. When he returned he was smiling. It wasn't "a great job" or "howdy" kind of smile, but one that said "you're fucked."

"You're in such deep shit right now. Austin wants me to bring you straight to him. I'd be prepared to have my ass kicked if I were you."

"If he kicks my ass hard enough, I won't be able to return the favor you asked of me."

Phil frowned.

"And if Stacy waits much longer, I'm going to sic Dallas on you."

When they landed—no other way to term what they were doing when flying like they were through the air—Austin was waiting. Phil stepped between the two of them and started to explain. "You should see the pictures that Connor has before you decide to kill him. It might make what we've done seem less stupid."

Austin growled. "I seriously doubt it. But come inside. If I have to kick both your asses, I don't want anyone to see."

Connor didn't think he'd be able to kick them both, but he knew his brother well enough to know that he'd try. CJ came out on the porch just as they stepped up on it. She looked upset. He asked her why and she cried as she told him.

"There was a pack attack this morning. Ten wolves killed and twenty more injured. The council is now in our living room."

Austin turned to him. "This have anything to do with the wolf in the cell Phil brought back?"

Connor nodded.

"Am I going to get my ass in deep because of it?"

Connor shook his head. "They'll probably reward you for finding it. I'm sorry, Austin, but there was no other way."

Austin nodded and they all went inside. The council of five was sitting around the table and their mom was feeding them. It was going to be a long day.

CHAPTER 4

The all-call was sounded about ten minutes ago and Stacy was not sure if she should go or stay away. She did not feel a part of Austin's pack, though it was not his fault, but she was not sure what to do. She decided to go, but to stay back in the event she was not needed.

The pack met once a month during the moon phase. She had never missed a meeting, but seldom ran with them. She was afraid someone would attack because she was not like them. Today, she knew that something had happened.

Austin started off by talking about the woman and her children. He told them that she wasn't safe where she'd been and he was asking that no one told where she was. Stacy knew that most of the pack would rather die than to disappoint him. Then he started talking about where she had come from.

"The alpha from where this woman had been attacked, attacked a smaller pack this morning. He killed more than half the males and took several of their females, some of them small yet. His name is Rich Sterling. If anyone sees a strange alpha on the grounds, contact someone in this house immediately. We will not allow him to do what he has done to another."

"Should we double the patrols around the grounds?" someone shouted from the back of the crowd. "What of our own families? Should we do something more to keep them out of harm's way?"

"I don't think so, but if you would feel safer for them to be put some place, bring them here. I have plenty of room and if we run low on room, we can bunk up some of the others until this is over." Austin conferred with his brother Connor. "Tighter patrols as well as more of you on a shift will be a good idea. Connor said he'd put up a list to see who wants to help out. I don't foresee him coming here so fast, but he will come."

Stacy waited for Austin to announce that she was Sterling's daughter and tensed every time he spoke. When she felt someone come near her, she thought they were there to take her to the front to be stoned.

"Hi." Connor stood next to her, but didn't touch. "I was wondering if you could help me with something. I want to see what you can tell me about Sterling. Do you know if he has any bolt holes, maybe a stash hidden somewhere? Anything you know could help us."

"I have not been there in many years. He might have something now that I would not be aware of." She moved forward and sniffed him. "I know that scent. You have been to see him."

She started to run, but he grabbed her arm. "No. I've been to the compound, but I didn't go near him. And for the record, I think the guy needs to be hung by his nuts and left there to die." She didn't move and he let go of her arm. "I have your uncle, Harvey. Do you remember him?"

She nodded. "I thought…I had heard he was dead. That after his family died he killed himself as well."

"No, but he's close. Did you know that Sterling killed his family? Murdered his mate while she was still carrying?" Stacy looked away. "Stacy, we need your help and no one here is going to harm you."

She decided to ignore the first part and to only answer what she had to of the second. "So the rumors were true. I had heard that my father had—"

"Don't call him that. He's not your father. Your sire maybe, but never your father." He gentled his voice then. "You were saying that Sterling had done something, what was it?"

She nodded, too overwhelmed with gratitude to say more. After a few minutes, she was able to continue. "I had heard that he had wanted my uncle's mate. And when he found out that she was breeding he went a little mad. He is said to have raped her and then gave her to anyone who would have her. She died giving birth to a stillborn. My uncle was to bury her with the others."

"But he didn't, did he? Where is she? Do you know?"

She nodded.

"Your uncle visits her, I would imagine."

"He does, or so I heard, until his...I was to say until his death, but... You say you have him? Does he need anything, sir? I have little, but I could give him what I have if it would help to keep him safe."

"He's safe and no harm will come to him. Will you see if you can talk to him? It would help us a great deal if we knew what we were going against."

She did not think it would do any good, but she told him she would try.

"Thank you Stacy. You've no idea how much this is going to help."

She went with him to the prison. They also had cells below ground in the event that a vampire were to come on the property and needed to be secured. Her uncle was in one of these cells. Connor told her it was so that the alpha could not contact him.

He looked so old, her uncle did. He was also very thin. She knew that at one time he had been a robust man, but now he was a shell of the person she once knew. He looked at her when she and Connor came to the cell door. "Do you know who I am?"

He didn't answer, but turned back to staring at the floor.

"I am your niece, Stacy O'Brien. My mother was—"

"He killed her too." She nodded and he continued without looking up. "My Mary too, and our babe. He said that she led him on and she hadn't. I knew my mate loved me."

"Yes, she did. She was so proud to be having your cub. She told me that she hoped for a son." Stacy felt Connor move back and the door was suddenly opened. She stepped in the room. "How have you been, Uncle Harvey?"

"I'd like to know if they could get me something. Do you think someone could bring me something to ease the memories?"

She knew he'd been on drugs; his entire body smelled of them.

"It'd be nice not to remember so much."

"I'll see what I can do. Uncle, do you know anything about what happened this morning? When Rich attacked the other pack?" She saw him stiffen.

"He made me go even though I've no will to live. I didn't hurt anyone, hoping that he'd...he has killed so many since my Mary. But he didn't." He looked up at her again. "Do you think I could have something to ease my memories, love? They hurt all the time."

Her heart broke for the man. He was barely there and she wanted to cradle him into her arms. When she moved forward Connor pulled her back with a shake of his head. "Scent," he whispered and let her go.

He did not want her to smell like him in case someone recognized it. She nodded and kneeled down to speak to her uncle. The tears in her eyes fell and she barely noticed them. "Are you telling me that Sterling led the attack this morning on those people?" He nodded. "But why? What did they do to him?"

"He wants to have her die by his hand. He won't allow anyone to leave without him saying its fine. No one ever leaves. Then I must do clean up for them. I have several holes that I've had to cover." He leaned back, took out a small notebook, and handed it out to her. Connor took it. "I had to draw a map so I wouldn't dig in the same place twice. So many dead."

She watched Connor thumb through the notebook and felt his anger as he gave it back to her. Then her uncle spoke again and the hair on her arms stood up.

"He's going to come for you too when he realizes I didn't kill you when I should have. I couldn't do it so I took you to another pack. They were to raise you as their own, but they didn't, did they?"

"I survived. I survived because of you."

He nodded then closed his eyes. "I would like something for the memories, please. Do you think someone could bring it to me soon?"

~~~

Dallas watched Connor and Stacy walk away together. He couldn't leave Austin's side, but he wanted to. He wanted to hunt his brother down and beat the shit out of him. His wolf agreed with him. He looked at Austin when he called the meeting to an end. He was off the platform before Austin could tell him to go.

He found them coming out of the cells. He didn't even ask, but hit Connor as hard as he could, knocking him back several feet. Connor was up in a second and coming at him. Stacy stepped between them at the last second and he hit her instead.

"Mother fuck, look what you've done. Christ, you've killed her." Connor tried to knock him away when he reached for her. "Leave her alone and I'll take her—"

"Touch her and you'll die." He knew his wolf had surfaced; his voice was rougher for it and his eyes had turned. "She's mine."

"Then fucking act like it. Claim her or I will." Connor stomped away and Dallas lifted her into his arms. When she moaned slightly his heart ached.

Dallas took her back to his home. He put her on his bed and went to get a wet cloth. He'd hit her hard and knew she'd been hurting when she woke. He wiped gently at the blood on her lip and hoped she'd forgive him in the next several lifetimes. When she opened her eyes he thought he'd be lucky if she gave him until hell froze over before she even spoke to him.

"You hit me."

He nodded, picked her up in his arms, and took her to the bathroom.

"I am quite capable of walking. Put me down please."

"I'm running you a tub. Then I'm going to help you bathe. I don't want you to be angry with me." She stiffened, but he didn't stop where he was going. "My sister says a bath can cure any kind of hurts."

"Then give her one. I wish to leave. Right now."

He didn't answer her. When the water was full enough, he turned it off and began to unbutton her blouse.

"What do you think you are doing?"

"You can't bathe in your clothes. They'll get wet and you'll have nothing to put back on." He grinned. "Not that you'll need it for a while, but eventually you need something."

She slapped at his hands and started to button the thing back up. Dallas let her go so far then he took the two ends and ripped it open. He nearly swallowed his tongue when he saw what she had on under it. Running his fingers over the soft silk, he heard her breath catch. The dark blue fabric barely held her in and her nipples were hard beneath it. He leaned down and took one hard peak into his mouth.

"Dallas, you cannot."

He lifted her onto the counter and broke the clasp off her bra. Her breasts spilled out and into his hands. When she leaned back on the counter he feasted on them. Licking one, then the other he couldn't decide which he wanted more so he lifted them together and took them both. Her fingers lacing in his hair had him groaning. When she started to unbutton his own shirt he told her to rip it and was satisfied when he heard it tear and buttons bounce all over the bathroom.

He pulled her pants off with her panties and shoes and stepped back. Christ, if there was anything more beautiful in the world, he'd like to know what it was. But he couldn't touch her just yet. "I want you. Right now, I want to take you as mine. But if you don't want me, now would be the time to say so." She was panting and her eyes had turned. "Stacy, tell me you want me as much as I do you."

"Yes," she hissed at him, and he stepped between her legs and took her mouth. When she whimpered he licked the sore and felt as if his body snapped into place. His mate. Stacy really was his mate.

"Say it. Tell me you're mine." He opened his pants and pulled them off. He stood before her naked and needy. "Say it, Stacy. Tell me what we both know."

"I'm your mate. I've waited for you for so long. But—"

He cut her off by taking her mouth again. As he picked her up, she wrapped her legs around his hips. With every step he took her pussy rubbed against his cock. If she kept this up he'd be coming over her and not in her. When he felt the bed touch his shins he laid them both down and covered her.

"I would like nothing more than to make slow love to you, but I need to claim you. I'll try and make it good for you, baby, but I've needed you for too long. Will you forgive me?"

"Please," she begged him, and he felt a calmness blanket him. Yes, he thought, he'd please her. She was his mate and deserved it from him. Untangling her legs from his hips he stood near the bed. He dropped to the floor and pulled her to the edge.

Without a word, he licked her from gate to clit and felt her rise from the bed for more. Taking as much of her as he could, Dallas felt his wolf calm too. He might just make it after all.

Loving her with his mouth, he reached up and pulled on her nipples. When she cried out he nearly stood and entered her, but if she came first he'd not hurt her as badly. When he felt her tighten around him, her thighs grip his head, he lifted her hands and put them to her breasts. She began squeezing them and pulling on her nipples as he had.

"Come for me, baby. Flood my mouth with your come." She arched up off the bed and screamed out her release. Even as he lapped at her he wanted to bite. *But not yet,* his wolf said. *Fuck her first then mark her.* As she came again he moved up her body, pulling her with him. He had her in the center of the bed when he fisted his cock at her entrance.

"It will hurt, love. I'm sorry, but it'll hurt." She pulled his head down to hers and kissed him. He knew that she had to taste herself on his mouth and her moan confirmed it.

"Take me. Mark me, please." She wrapped her feet around his thighs and lifted her pussy up to his cock. "Please, Dallas, fill me."

He couldn't wait any longer. As soon as he entered her sheath she cried out again, this time he knew from pain. He stilled. As much as he wanted to pound into her he knew that he'd better pull out and try again. When she moved he moaned, and when she smiled he nearly came.

"Baby, I can't hurt you anymore, but if you move like that again I won't be able to be a gentleman and pull out."

"You pull from my body now, Dallas Force, and I will hurt you." She moved again and he couldn't help moving too. "More. Please give me more."

He tried to be slow, but she wouldn't have it. When she nuzzled his neck and licked his vein he nearly let go. But he needed to feel her come again. When he leaned down and took her breast into his mouth she moved her lips over his throat. Suddenly, she nipped at him he felt his climax race through him. He did the only thing he could do, he bit her. And her biting him had him fall over the edge.

He dropped his weight down onto her. She giggled and he looked up at her. She was the most beautiful person he'd ever seen and she was his.

"Giggling is not kind, love. You should know that wolves take lovemaking very seriously and a giggling female isn't very nice." He kissed her quickly before he turned to his back, taking her with him. She sat up over him and his cock surged to life again.

"You are not finished, are you? Oh Dallas, that was so much fun that we have to do it again." She rolled her body over his until her pussy was over his hardening cock. "Show me how to pleasure you the way you did me with my mouth. I loved that."

His cock went from semi-hard to straining to be where she wanted it in seconds. He thought he could reason with her about taking her virginity and being sore. But she scooted down his body and took him into her mouth.

"Christ," he bellowed. Her mouth was hot and wet and he nearly came again when she gagged around him. Guiding her to where she couldn't hurt either of them, he told her what he needed. "Lick me from the root to the tip. That's it. When you take me into your mouth, you should—Christ, Stacy, that's it."

She pulled him deep in her throat and swallowed. His cock surged up and he felt her touch his balls. His climax was close again and he came when she cupped his balls into her hot hand. It was over much too quickly, but he was sure he'd have died if she had much more in the way of lessons. Pulling her up to his chest he flipped her to her back and settled between her thighs.

"You look like you could eat me alive." Her voice was rough and sexy. "Are you going to, Dallas?"

"Yes. Then I'm going to mark you again. This time I want to taste your blood. I want us bonded as well as mated before you leave this room." She nodded to him. "Will you bond with me, Stacy? Be mine forever?"

"Yes. Tell me what to do. I know that I must draw blood, but…when do I do it?"

"When we climax together." He nearly came when she smiled again. "When we climax together, we'll bite together.

You bite my throat and I'll bite you. Understand?" She nodded. "This is forever, baby. I'm never letting you go."

She touched her finger to his cheek. "I know. And I'm ready."

He entered her slowly, knowing she'd be sore. But he couldn't do that pace for long. Moving in and out of her was amazing and he found that she was meeting him stroke for stroke when he felt her wolf stir against his.

When she let her wolf go a little he felt his own wolf respond. Her canines were sharp and Dallas couldn't wait to feel them sink into his flesh. As soon as she came he came again. They let their wolves mark each other as their human selves marked as well. The second her blood entered his mouth and his into hers he knew they were one. Stacy Force was his mate.

KATHI S. BARTON

CHAPTER 5

Rich called again and received the same message. "I can't come to my phone right now, but if you leave a message I'll get back with you as soon as I can." He threw the fucking phone across the room. Where the fuck was his butler?

He'd gone back outside to let him retire for the night and couldn't find him. Rich had actually forgotten about Harvey until he'd been about to go to bed. And other than the door to his car being open there was no sign of him anywhere. Rich had shouted for him for nearly an hour before he'd gone up to bed thinking he'd simply gotten high again and wandered off. But this morning the limo was still in the drive and the door still hung open. And there was no sign of Harvey ever being there, only the faint scent of heroin in the car. It was as if he'd vanished.

Trying to remember where his brother lived proved futile. All he knew was he showed up every day and left every day. And Rich wasn't going to go out and ask anyone where he lived. Not for any amount of money. He did, however, call to see if anyone from the tight group his brother had hung around with had seen him.

"No, sir. I can go to his home and see if…well, if maybe he's taken too much this time. The man never knew his limit."

That was true and Rich laughed. Of course few knew that he gave him the drugs or that he was his brother, but that was neither here nor there. "You do that. And send me someone to take over his duties until we know for sure. I need someone to drive me to the meeting in town." He heard the hesitation, but the man finally said he'd send someone over. Rich knew that he'd have a hard time of it and found that he didn't care. Soon someone would be here and he'd have his breakfast made and things would be back to normal.

The phone ringing had him jump and, when he could get his heart back under control, he picked it up. There wasn't any time for him to say even his name before someone began to speak.

"They know the conditions you keep your wolves in and the council is coming to investigate. If I were you I'd leave now and avoid being put into prison. It's not a place for you." The line went dead and he laid it gently back into the cradle.

He sat there for several more seconds before he stood up and looked around. *Now what?* his mind screamed at him. He had to leave, but to where? No one would take him in and he doubted very much he'd want to live in any of the "houses" he had provided for them. He went to his safe and opened it.

He would need money. Lots of it too. Taking out the three large bags, he set them on the floor, went to the safe on the other side of the room, and took out what was there as well. He was taking the second load to the car when he realized that the battery was dead. Going to the garage, he opened the trunk to the first car he saw and started putting his bags into it. That's when he heard the car pull up. He hid behind the car and watched as they looked into the last bag he'd yet to bring with him.

"He's bolting. Maybe he's still in the house and we'll be able to bring him in."

Rich didn't know these two, but was willing to bet that they were not his replacement enforcer. The men went inside as another car pulled up.

The larger man came out of the house and shook hands with the other three new arrivals. "He's not inside, but he's not been gone long. He left some of his ill-gotten gains behind." The newcomers walked to the money and kicked the bag. Rich found himself nearly going out to them to kick them when he realized he'd never come out the victor with these men. They were well taken care of.

He sniffed the air wondering if it were possible to get their scent. He nearly screamed out when he smelled vampire, and the other man was an alpha too. He tightened in to where he hid and waited. He knew that the new council that was forming to take care of both weres and vampire had one of each on the board. He wondered if these two knew who they were.

This was an ambush. Someone wanted his territory and this was how they were going to get it. It never occurred to him that he'd done the same to get the one he was in, but that didn't seem relative right now. These men were on his property. But he wasn't going to confront them just yet. He was desperate, but not stupid.

"I say we gather up all we can here and see if we can get some of his pack to come with us. They can't be happy here and, if he's abandoned his position, I'm well within my rights to take it."

One of the newcomers agreed. "You should call them to you. I've a report that says he's only got about sixty left. Shame, too. This was a very large pack at one time. Too bad the younger wolves have no pride in their responsibilities."

Rich knew that voice. It was the man he'd spoken to earlier in the week.

"You call them to you and while I'm here I'll witness their coming to you."

Rich knew that not one person would leave him. He'd been threatening them enough with death that they'd be terrified out of their minds to leave. He sat down to wait for the first of them to tell this person that they'd rather stay here.

When the bell rang for the meeting place it only took them several minutes to come. Rich had trained them on that as well. Promptness was all he would tolerate. He was surprised at how few came and realized that the pompous ass had been right. There were very few people in his pack.

"I'm Austin Force, alpha of the Force pack. I've seen how you're living and have come to offer you refuge in my pack. You will pledge to me now and I'll make sure that your living conditions change immediately."

No one moved just as he'd expected. But the alpha wasn't finished it seemed. Rich wasn't worried. These people would be stupid to leave and some of them had seen what he would do.

"I believe your alpha has left you. The council is here to arrest him and take him into custody for crimes against our kind. I am well within my rights to simply take you under my protection, but I would rather you came of your own free will."

"What of our families? Will you murder them if we do not do as you say?"

Rich almost popped his head up to see who had spoken, but didn't at the last minute. He'd find the prick and burn him alive.

"I wouldn't do that even if you yourself had committed the most heinous crime. Family is all we have and I never hurt them. My mother would skin me alive." There was a small laugh from the group and more questions were asked.

The man was a sap if even half of what he was saying was true.

"Yes, there are houses. Not enough if you all come now, but we'll figure something out in the meantime. But we've plenty of food. Each house is yours so long as you want and your families are only required to give what you can. And I never take more than we can use."

"How do we know what you say is true?"

Take that, Rich thought.

"How do we know that once you get us to where you say you're taking us, you don't kill us?"

"If we wanted you dead, you'd be there already." This was from the vampire. "Austin Force is my brother-in-law and friend. As a vampire I will have you know that, if he wanted you dead, I would have killed you all before the first of you fell to the earth."

There were some mummers of voices, but nothing Rich could make out. Then he heard something large pull into the drive. He looked over the trunk of his car and saw two large city buses sitting there. What the hell was this?

"If you want to come with me this is the only time I will bring you a ride. After this you'll have to get to me on your own. I have two doctors on each bus and they will tend to your needs. If at any time you want to leave my pack, then you are more than free to go. But again, you leave on your own."

Rich laughed to himself. The man really was a sap. Providing transportation, doctors, and that stupid speech was enough to make him sick. The man would be lucky if one person got on either bus. He pulled out his cell phone and listened to his music with the headphones he had in his pocket to drown out the insidious noise of the idiots. He knew without a doubt that this man was wasting his time. He'd not been easy on these people and there was no way they'd make a break for it now.

After an hour his battery died. He heard the engines start and then the crunch of the gravel just as he was putting the now dead phone in his pocket. Any minute now he'd go out and see his pack standing like sheep waiting for him to tell them to go home. Rich straightened his clothes and stood up. Time to tell the sheep to leave.

The drive was empty. The limo was there, of course, but there were no people. Even his bag of money was missing. He thought maybe they'd gone home already, left the alpha to stand there alone with his big rides, but he didn't know. He was about to go back to his car when he saw the paper waving under the wiper blade. He took it off and read it.

"That's how a real alpha treats his subjects. He doesn't do it by hiding in the garage crouched behind a car like a small child afraid of his own shadow. Signed, Austin Force." The post script had him snarling. *"By the way, I have Georgia and her cubs."*

He tore the note up and then shifted, tearing his clothes from his body. He was going to kill someone and he didn't care who. The first person he saw had better have their things in order because they were as good as dead.

~~~

Dallas stood outside the studio and tried to think how to do this. He knew Alexis had heard about him hitting Stacy, but he didn't know how she'd take it. He also knew that she and Stacy were good friends despite being alpha to a pack. He didn't knock, but walked in.

The slap startled him. It was hard and drew blood to his lip. Before he could reach up to wipe off the blood Alexis started in on him. Dallas was too stunned at first to do more than stand there.

"How could you? How could you hit a woman?" He started to speak, but she snarled at him. "Don't you dare try to justify it. I know what happened. You hit her and knocked her out. Do you know what's it like to lose a connection like that? To not know what happened to the person you can no longer hear?"

He stood there for several seconds wondering if she was finished, his own anger nasty and hot. When she turned to him she drew back her hand to hit him again. He grabbed it before she could connect.

"Once was quite enough. I hit her, yes, but she walked into a fist that was meant for another." She started to speak and he held up his hand. "When you injure a man for no reason, he gets to—"

"No reason," she shouted at him. "I suppose you find it all right to hit someone that's much smaller than you."

"No, I don't. But had she not, then I wouldn't have bonded with her, nor become her mate." She took a step back. "In my family we ask before judging. I'm sorry you have so little faith in me that you'd…that you'd hit then not ask questions." He turned to leave.

"Don't, Dallas. I didn't know. I—"

"No, you didn't. Nor did you ask." He walked out the door, shutting it quietly behind him. He was nearly naked by the time the door opened and he was almost to the forest line when she came out of the building.

By the time he'd been out for nearly three hours he knew that he'd have to apologize to her. He'd been wrong to walk away from her. Males didn't treat the females in their family like he'd done. He moved along the perimeter of the land to the furthest part and sat down near a spring and closed his eyes. He felt a small touch of someone trying to contact him and ignored it. Right now he didn't want to speak to anyone.

He had a mate. Not just any mate either, but Stacy O'Brien. She was everything he'd hoped for in a mate and then some. And she was all his. He smiled as his wolf stretched. Both their beasts were happy as well.

"How long you going to be out there before you come back home?"

He could ignore everyone else, including his mate, but not his alpha. *"I might not. I think I'll collect my mate and live as a wolf for the rest of our days."* He heard his brother laugh. *"I'm not kidding, Austin. I'm not in the mood for your lecture. When I've cooled off enough I'll do my duty and apologize to her, but I'm not even close to making it sincere right now."*

"What if I told you she is crying because she feels she hurt you? What if—"

"I don't care and she did hurt me. Leave it be, please. I don't want to talk about it or her." Dallas stood up and stretched and then walked to the water's edge.

"Dallas, it's not the way you think it is. Gordon is upset with her and Stacy won't even speak to her. Everyone is pissed at her, not you."

He snorted at his brother.

"I'm not lying to you. She's been crying since she came to me over two hours ago and is, as we speak, telling anyone who will listen that she is a monster that hits without thinking."

He wanted that to feel good, but he felt horrible about it. He started back toward the pack house without speaking to his brother. It didn't seem to matter to him. Austin seemed to be in a talkative mood.

"Mom isn't happy either, but I can't tell if she's just mad at the whole thing, you, or Alexis. She's baking."

That stopped him in his tracks.

She's made more cookies and cupcakes than I think we'll be able to eat in the next five moon phases."

"I didn't hit Stacy on purpose. And she and I mated and bonded last night." He started moving again when he had to stop again. *"Austin, have you been in the south fields this week?"*

"No. What do you see?"

He could hear the tension in his voice and it made the hair on the back of his neck rise.

"Dallas, speak to me."

"I can smell...death. Not fresh, but...older. Let me look around and get back to you."

"No. You keep in contact. After yesterday I don't want to take any chance with anyone. You said you're in the south field. Where?"

He told him.

"I'm coming. Don't look around, just wait for me."

"Austin. It's too late. I've found it."

By the time Austin got to where he was Dallas had shifted and pulled on the sweats that he had on him. Since his brother Connor had told them it was easy to carry a small pack on their backs when they were wolf, one that he'd designed that had breakaway straps, all of them were able to dress wherever they went. He was standing over the mass grave when Austin and Myles came up in a Jeep.

"I didn't know what to bring so we loaded everything we could think of." Myles was an ex-cop and a newly turned vampire thanks to Phil and Holly saving him. "You figure out what it is yet?"

"You tell me." He led them over to the shallow grave and pointed. "Male, female, human, animal, weres, and vampires. I'm not sure on the last one whether or not it's a vamp, though. The only dead vamps I've seen were ash and this one is not."

"Christ," Austin hissed. Dallas had to agree. "They look like they've been here at least a week. How deep is this thing, would you say?"

Dallas knew. "There are seventeen bodies. No children are in there, but someone was kind enough to put all the adults' identifications in that box there."

Myles walked over to it and opened the steel box. He was thumbing through a wallet as Dallas continued.

"Stacy and Connor spoke to Harvey today. He said that he was responsible for burying the dead that Sterling killed. I didn't look at the book, but he gave it to Stacy and she said it had all the places that he'd dug up. He didn't want to go to the same place twice."

"So Sterling has been keeping track, or at least someone is. This Harvey, how does he figure in all this?"

Dallas shrugged at Myles' question.

"Do you think he's in with the alpha?"

Another Jeep pulled up and someone walked toward them speaking. "No, he's not. The alpha is his brother and killed his family in order to keep him in line. Harvey is under the impression that he's nothing left to live for. Hello, Dallas. You can't know how sorry I am for all this."

Dallas turned away from his brother Connor. He wasn't too happy with him either.

"What took you so long?" Austin looked around when another car pulled up. "What the hell did you do, bring the entire pack with you?"

"No, just the ones I thought could help."

Phil came toward them as well as Holly. Dallas didn't want her to see this, but she walked right up to the dead and hopped down in the hole. "This one was killed with a knife.

I'd say a dagger. This one on top...looks like a nine millimeter." She moved along each body and told them how they'd been killed and about how long they'd been dead. All of them less than a week.

"I'd say there are two vampires in that mess, maybe one more, but no more than that. And they weren't dead when they were put in here, but died due to sun exposure." Phil winked at his mate. "I think they might not be day walkers like me."

"Ass," she growled at him. "All the others were killed someplace else and brought here. I'd say that they were carried, so that would explain why there are no other tire tracks." She got out of the hole. "There's something else you should know. The person on the bottom, the male, he dug the hole."

"How do you know? Are there some markings that gave that away?" Dallas flushed when she cocked a brow at him. "I'm sorry. I'm having a shitty day."

"Yeah, heard about that." She grinned. "Anyway, the guy still has the shovel in his hands. Wrapped around it like he was still in mid-dig when he was shot in the back of the head."

Holly was a former hit man...woman for the government. When she'd retired Connor, Myles, and she opened an investigations firm. Their business had been doing very well. In fact, they now had any other member of the family working for them when they were too busy to do it on their own. Dallas didn't much care for his sister being anything but a mate, but he knew better than to say anything.

"Let's get them out of here and call whoever we need to so they can get claimed." Dallas pulled out his cell phone as he walked away. "I'm calling the were brigade to see what they can do for us."

Eight hours later they were just heading back. Dallas wanted to do nothing more than take a long, hot shower and crawl into bed. He was met at the door by not only Alexis, but Stacy, his mom, and CJ, who grinned at him.

"We have to talk."

Christ, would this day never end?

CHAPTER 6

"The council said that Sterling has been a problem for some time. But as they didn't have any proof they decided to wait." Austin was pacing as he spoke. He had his family sitting around the large pack table and couldn't seem to think past the bodies in the grave.

"Why? I mean, I've been there. How can they not think the guy is abusing his people?" Connor handed out the pictures that he'd shown Austin when he'd gotten back. "Those alone should show that he's not a good pack leader."

"But the council didn't see those places." He tossed a folder on the table. "They saw those houses. With clean, well fed people in them. People who couldn't say enough good things about their leader."

He watched them spread the pictures on the table and see what they'd been told. When Austin had tried to tell the council what he'd heard from Georgia he'd been reprimanded for taking in another wolf's fold without permission. After today they had a different story.

"So what do they think now? Do we go in and...shit. Look at this picture." Phil tossed the picture in the middle of the table and then stood up. He went to the file that still lay on the counter. "Yeah, I thought so. It's the same woman. Here."

Phil pointed to the woman in the front door to a very lovely two-story home and then to the driver's licenses they'd found in the box. It was the same woman. And her identification said she was from this area.

"Is he taking people from other packs and setting them up in these homes…to what? Make a good impression? Then he kills them off when they've done what he needed?" No one answered Myles. "That's just sick. Not only that, but isn't there some sort of pack law that prohibits abuse of your subjects?"

"Very good, grasshopper," Phil said sardonically. "That's pretty much the law for any group or species. When our kind is caught treating people like this he's staked to the ground, pissed on, and then watched from a safe distance as the sun takes care of him or her."

Myles flushed. "Sorry. Still thinking like a cop. What I don't understand is how did he know to set this up? Did they tell him they were coming?"

Austin nodded. "Pretty much. It's considered 'uncivilized' to go to a pack without announcing yourself."

Austin noticed that Stacy was looking at the pictures with more interest than he thought necessary. When she looked up at Dallas he knew they were talking and wondered if it was something they all should know. When Dallas nodded she turned to him.

"I know where this is. It's about four or five miles from where the bodies were found." She looked down at the picture with the woman in the doorway. "This is someone I've seen on this land. She said she wasn't poaching, but she was just…she said she had gotten lost. I thought she was afraid, but she left before I could speak to her about it."

"When did you see her? It would help, love, if you could remember."

Everyone looked at Dallas who had growled low to the vampire when he'd asked.

"Oh sorry. I keep forgetting how possessive you wolves can be. Would it help if I said 'Where did you see her, bitch, tell me now?'" Phil shook his head. "Morons."

"Oh like you blood suckers aren't. And that's my mate you're calling "love" and I'd appreciate it if you'd back the fuck up."

No one spoke. Austin had forgotten that Dallas had found his mate and, now that he thought about it, he realized that Alexis hadn't spoken a word since they sat down.

"Ah, so that's what's so different about you. My deepest apologizes to you, kind sir. Congratulations, my dear lady, though I think you could have done much better." Phil took Dallas' hand and shook it. "I am sorry, but it is a bad habit I have."

"You can call me whatever you want if it will get us back to the subject at hand. I—"

"Wait. I have something to say as well." Alexis stood up. "I owe everyone here a heartfelt apology as well. I wronged Dallas today and I was cruel and heartless to him. I also hit him."

Austin watched the room around him, especially Gordon and Dallas. This could be bad or it could be extremely bad.

"He came to me today to tell me that he'd hit Stacy and that he and she had bonded. I acted like a banshee and I acted without getting all the facts. I hope that you both can forgive me."

Dallas stood, as did Gordon. Neither man moved for several seconds until Gordon sat down. Dallas moved to Alexis, knelt before her, and took her hand into his. He kissed her gently and Austin held his breath. Okay, very bad to completely fucked up now.

"I'm sorry too. I should have come to you immediately to tell you what had happened. But…" Dallas looked at Stacy, who flushed. "But I got sidetracked. Will you please forgive me as well?"

She started crying and helped him stand, then wrapped her arms around him. Dallas looked a Gordon, who nodded once before Dallas wrapped his arms around her. They held each other for a few minutes before Gordon slapped him on the shoulder.

"Don't push your luck. Let go of my mate." They parted and each of them hugged Gordon before Dallas went to his seat, but didn't sit.

"This is my mate, Stacy Force. We have bonded and mated in the way of our people. Alpha, I know it's a little late, but may I take a mate and, Alexis, may I take a mate in Stacy?"

Austin sat down and nodded. Alexis said, "hell yes" as he let out a long held breath. Things in this family were never going to be dull. He looked over at his own mate and pulled her into his lap.

"I call this meeting back to order. Tell us what you've found, Connor." Austin watched the play between the other couples and wondered when Connor would find his true love. He nearly missed what Stacy said.

"What do you mean you've met all these wolves? On this property?"

She nodded.

"Why wasn't I made aware of it?"

"They were only on the outer edges. You said that so long as they didn't move into the perimeter it would be fine if others came close."

He nodded. Damn it, they'd made that rule hoping to interact with others of their kind when they'd taken over this land. Now he might have to rethink it. "But how close to the dig site did they come? Any of them within the five miles from the Sterling boarder?"

He saw her thinking and then she nodded. "But not much more, if that. Most of them were…they seemed to think that you were going to kill them. At least the first few." She looked thoughtful again. "You don't think they were trying to get away, do you?"

More than likely, he thought. "I want to expand the patrols to all around the perimeter. Whatever we find, report. I know we've absorbed the pack into ours, but we can't take the chance that he'll come gunning for them." Austin actually hoped he would. That was why he'd left the note. He wanted to make sure he came. And when he entered his territory, he was as good as dead.

~~~

Dallas was dead on his feet. When Stacy had gotten them home. He'd been dozing in the car when she finally pulled into his driveway. She really was nervous about what to do now. She reached over to touch his shoulder and he jerked awake and grabbed her hand.

"It's me. It is all right. It is just me." His breathing calmed and she could feel the tension go out of his body. "Are you all right?"

"I'm exhausted. I'm sorry, love, to have made you drive home, but I couldn't have made it." He opened the door and she sat there. "Aren't you coming in?"

She looked at his house, one she had been in a thousand times over the past year, and then at him. "I do not know what to do. Do I live here? Do I go to the house that I have? I do not know how this is supposed to work."

He closed the door and looked at her. "You're my mate Stacy and, as of now, we live together. Forever. I thought you understood that."

"I did. I do. But what…are you sure?" She hated to sound whiny, but she was afraid he would get tired of her and want her to leave or, worse yet, he would beat her. Well, that really was not something she was concerned about, but she was afraid.

"I've never been surer of anything in my life. I need you. I love you. I want to spend the rest of our lives together." He kissed her forehead. "Does this have anything to do with your father?"

"He said those same things to Mom before he killed her. He told her that he would never tire of her, never leave her. I do not want to lose you, but…well, I do not know what you expect of me."

"I don't either other than to love me back. I do expect you to tell me if I do something that pisses you off. I expect you to tell me when you're not satisfied." She flushed at his statement. "I meant in the house, the car, whatever. But I don't expect you'll have any complaints about me satisfying you. I'm a phenomenal lover, as you already know."

She pretended to think about it and squeaked when he yanked her over the seat and onto his lap. She was straddled over his legs and he held her to him. She was sure he was asleep when she pulled back, but his eyes were wide open.

"I love you, Dallas. I think I have for a long time." She laid her head on his. "And if you take me inside your house, I will show you."

The swat at her ass hurt and she yanked his head back, ready to take a bite out of him. Before she could speak, he hit her again. Then he began rubbing the bruised area.

"Our house. Say it. Our house. Our bed. Our car." He licked her throat. "Our bodies. Say it so I can take you inside our house and make love to you on our bed."

She kissed his nose. "Our house." Then his eye. "Our car." Then the other one. "Our bodies." She leaned back on his lap.

"You forgot our bed."

She leaned down and kissed him full on the mouth, putting her entire being into it. "No, I did not. Take me there and I will prove it."

He opened the door and set her out of the car. When he slid out as well he turned her to the vehicle and set her on it.

"It's much too far. What if I show you how much we own this car?" He pulled her to the edge and nipped at her mouth. "Out here where we are among out kind. Where we were meant to make love."

He pulled her light jacket off and then pulled her shirt off and dropped it to the ground. While he bit at her neck she pulled him between her legs and wrapped herself around him. His low groan made her bold.

"I want to undress you then I want to take you into my mouth. I want to feel you inside of me." She ran her hands over his hard male nipples. "Do you have any idea how much I want to touch you right now?"

"I'm getting an idea."

She pushed him back and then turned him to the place she had been sitting.

"What is it you think you are going to do to me? I want to make love to you."

"My turn. You get to call the shots in the bed. Right here, right now, I'm going to be in charge." She looked up at him and saw his eyes darken. "Will you let me try?"

He nodded and leaned back on the car and let her undress him. First she unbuttoned his shirt, then she worked at his jeans. The button came undone, but the zipper was giving her fits. She looked up at him again and watched as she ripped the sucker off him.

"You're going to replace those. I love those pants." He grinned at her. "Of course I'm willing to let it go if you show me how sorry you are."

Dropping to her knees before him, she pulled his pants the rest of the way off. She left his boxers where they were, tossed the ruined jeans over her shoulder, and sat up on her knees so she could reach him. His cock was right where she wanted it.

Running her hands up his thighs then up over the elastic of the shorts, she watched him. Every time she came close to the head he would rock toward her mouth. She was not ready for that yet; she wanted to play. When he growled at her she felt her own juices begin to flow and rubbed her cheek over his shaft.

"I love the way you smell. Like rich earth and nature." She pulled the boxers down until just the crown was out and licked the very tip. "And you taste like…hum, like the best chocolate I've ever had."

"Stacy, please. A man can only take so much teasing." He wrapped his fingers into her hair. "Take me, baby. Please, I'm begging you."

She did take the tip into her mouth and worried the full head with her tongue. Pulling the boxers off while she took him, she left them at his knees to reach up and take his balls gently into her palms. His growl this time was punctuated with harsh breathing and a few "Holy Christs."

She lost herself in what she was doing. His taste, his texture. Never had she known how a part of the body could be so hard, yet remain so smooth. So hot, yet not burn when she touched him. When he pulled her head off his cock he looked crazed. She licked her lips and moved to take him again.

"Enough. I need to come or fuck you. I can't…Christ, you're going to kill me." He stood her up, pressed her head down on the hood, and he stepped up behind her. "You've made me insane with need. I hope to Christ you're ready."

She knew she was and, if she had not been, his rough words would have done the trick. As soon as her pants were ripped from her she felt his hand come down on her ass. Nothing in the world had ever felt this good and so painful at the same time.

"Take me. Now, Dallas, take me or, so help me, I will figure out a way to—mother fuck." He slammed into her deep. Her thighs were going to be bruised in the morning, but right now, all she could think about was him fucking her. Over and over he pounded into her. When he reached around to her pussy and pinched her clit she came apart with a scream.

"Again," he commanded. "Come again."

She felt her body tense for several seconds, then it came apart again. When he stiffened behind her, his cock so deep she could almost imagine it touching her womb, she came when he shouted out his own release. Even as her own climax jerked and took over every nerve-ending in her being, she felt him bite deep into her shoulder, the pain bringing another smaller, but no less fantastic, climax from her. When he dropped over her completely, his body limp against hers, she closed her eyes. As she drifted away, letting herself be pulled under, she thought about simply sleeping here for the rest of her life because there was no way she was going to be able to move again.

CHAPTER 7

His house was gone. Rich looked around the driveway and couldn't believe that someone would come here and burn his house to the ground. And the way it looked, not even the fire engines had been in. He kicked a wad of something and watched the ash scatter in the morning air. He was glad now that he'd not been home. What if he'd been inside when…well, he was reasonably sure that they would have wakened their leader. Then he frowned. There was no one left to save their leader.

There were some prints, but mostly, they were smeared and without substance. He was looking for paw prints or even booted prints, but there were none of those either. And the scent was just too smogged up with soot for him to smell any one thing. Then there was the added smell of all the things, furniture, clothes, as well as food in the pantry and kitchen that had burned as well.

The car coming up the drive had him jumping for shelter. After the past few days that he'd had, he was nearly afraid of his own shadow. Not that he'd admit that to anyone, but he wasn't going to look brave only to get killed for no reason. He was hiding behind a tree when he saw the unknown car pulling up. Humans.

"See, I told you it was a mess. I wonder who lived here." The female got out of the car and walked to the hood of the car. "It's creepy looking, isn't it?"

"Yeah, I guess. Tell me again why we're here. I thought you said you had something amazing to show me. This place looks like a dump."

Rich started to step forward and add to the dump by killing them both when he saw the gun in the man's pants.

"If we're going to get some miles behind us we should head out."

Rich thought about attacking them both and stealing their car. But after yesterday? He shuddered. No, he'd stay hidden until he could get a better grip on what the fuck was going on.

He'd been on a run and out for blood two days ago. Nothing, not even a stupid field mouse, was around. When he finally got to the lake at the other end of his property he'd had to lie down. It had been a long time, years he guessed, that he'd been out, much less on a run. Then when he'd been drinking from the water he got a good look at himself.

Dirty—no, that was too tame for what he'd been. Filthy. He'd been so filthy that he'd not even recognized himself. His eyes, usually a nice warm brown, were dark, black almost. His fur was matted and singed in places where he'd gotten too close to an electric fence. His left paw was sore where he'd walked on the road and it had been hotter than he'd thought. Then jumping out of the way of a large truck had him turning his right ankle. Even shifting last night hadn't eased the pain and he'd had to sleep in the outdoors. Someone was going to pay for this and he knew just who it was going to be.

Austin Force.

A man's name said so much about the person. His name, Sterling, was to him just what he'd wanted in a name. Authentic, real and true, of genuinely high quality. Excellent.

When he'd been looking for a name, something more than the name he'd been born with, he'd found several before he'd come across the word Sterling. It had served him well over the years and now it had followed him to pack leader. Unlike the name Force.

It gave the connotation of being strong, but when he'd looked it up he only saw what it could mean, to use against a person, as he was sure anyone would. Physical power to overcome or restrain a person. Physical coercion or violent physical power or strength exerted against a person. Everything that he'd ever want in a name. And as soon as the man was dead he'd take his name too.

And he was going to kill him. There was no doubt about that. As soon as he figured out where he was and where the fuck his brother was he was going to hunt him down, tear him limb from limb, and then bury him in a marked grave so that when he wanted, he could go there and taunt the bastard.

He thought about the fact that he'd stolen Georgia from him as well. The whiny bitch was probably right at this moment telling them things like, "Rich has starved me," "wouldn't let my children go to school when work needed to be completed," and more than likely that he'd killed her mate. All of this was true, but she had no right airing what had happened between his pack to another master. The engine starting brought him to the present.

The man was driving this time and Rich actually thought about attacking the female, but was still sore from yesterday. He limped out of his hiding place and watched them drive away, thinking how lucky they were that he wasn't up to par. He looked back at his house and wondered who he could blame for this and decided it might as well lay on the Force bastard's head. He made his way to the cave he'd spent a cold night in last night, cursing his fortune.

He had a great deal of money, thanks to his people. Laughing, he thought of all they'd given up for him to be a rich wolf. But without transportation, clean clothes, as well as even a cell phone to call for help, it might as well have been kindling. He walked into the darkened area and sat next to the pit he'd tried to build a fire in. He hadn't been able to get that going either and decided that Force was going to have a lot to account for when Rich caught up with him.

Closing his eyes he reached for Harvey again. There was nothing. As if he was hitting a hard wall. He knew his brother had to be suffering about now. He could barely go an hour without wanting something to ease his pain. *Some pain,* he thought nastily. The stupid man didn't even know the pain he was causing his brother right now. Rich looked at his ankle and decided that it was getting better. There hadn't ever been any swelling, nor had he had a bruise. He knew it had to have been broken or at least badly sprained. He wasn't going to admit, not even under threat of death, that he'd not really been hurt all that much, but hadn't been in the best of shape and thus had fallen. He'd admit that to himself sure, but not to anyone else.

Rich thought about his life. Not about his parents very much if he didn't have to. They'd died almost before he'd realized how worthless they'd been. Not even a pot to piss in, his brother used to say, but they'd been happy. Harvey was a sap too, he decided, and had probably overstayed his usefulness. It was time for someone new anyway.

No, he thought about his mate and child. Mostly his child. At the moment he couldn't recall her name, something common no doubt. But she'd been deformed, he remembered. And a deformity like hers made her not worthy of him being her father. How on earth would anyone want a child that had no scent?

Rich had blamed it on her mother. Nothing like that could have happened because to him, his genes were superior. Then there was the fact that he was sure his mate had lain with someone else and she'd done something during her whelping to make it so he'd never know. It was purely speculation on his part and probably not even possible, but it had made him mad when he'd heard one of the others speaking about it. The child hadn't even looked like him. Her fur was…well, he couldn't remember right now, but thought it was gray or something.

Of course, the man had been joking more than likely, but Rich hadn't liked the idea. Nor the man. He'd killed him first then everyone he could remember being in the room when the comment had been made so that no one would think his mate had stepped out on him. After that, killing for the pleasure had been something he found he became good at. And it helped him move up the ladder to where he was now. Actually, it was very easy.

"And see who's alpha now." He looked around the cave when his voice echoed around him. He knew he'd spooked himself, but didn't like the idea that it'd been so easy either. He was not going to be one of those people who went insane because things weren't going his way.

"Tomorrow," he whispered so that nothing would sound around him. "Tomorrow I'm going to go and find the prick, get back my property, and then rebuild. They'll come running back to me once I show them what a weak, spineless piece of shit that Austin Force is."

Closing his eyes, Rich smiled. Yes. He was back now. And he'd show all of them that, while he might have been down, he certainly wasn't out of the game yet. He frowned slightly. He would have to deal with the council, but if he tossed enough money their way…well, it was going to be very costly to put himself back where he belonged. But to see the look on their faces it would be well worth it.

~~~

Dallas awoke and reached his hand out for Stacy. Damn but he'd never slept so well. Opening one eye when he'd gotten nothing but cold sheets, he rolled to his back and was disappointed to find himself in the bed alone. He looked down at his hard cock and thought about what he'd have to do to his mate to ensure that she stayed in bed until he got up. Him, not his cock, though that had its merits too.

He could smell bacon frying and decided to go to the kitchen to get Stacy when he remembered that he still had guests. Three families were staying in his house until they could find them suitable homes in the area. Austin had thought that it would be a good time to expand the pack housing, but didn't know just how to begin. Dallas had a few contractors coming out today to see what they could do. Heading to the shower instead of the stairs, he took a quick one and was dressed in less than five minutes. He entered the kitchen, glad that he'd remembered the people as it looked as if they were helping put food on the table.

When the little girl saw him she dropped the plate she was holding and then dropped to the floor in the glass. He rushed to her only to have Stacy step in front of him.

"Slowly. These children are not used to strange big men who are nice to them." He looked at the little girl then back at Stacy as she spoke through their link. *"She is terrified you will send them back, as are the rest of them."*

Dallas nodded and walked slowly to her and helped her stand. He tried his best not to look at her. One glance at the terror in her eyes had him wanting to find the bastard who'd done this to them and pluck his fur out one follicle at a time.

"Here we go, little lady. No harm done. I didn't much care for these plates anyway. I think my brother gave them to me." Actually, his mother had and he knew she'd forgive him the lie. These were his favorite plates. "Let's see if you cut yourself when you fell."

Her legs looked like twigs. He figured she had to be at least seven or eight and should have strong legs and certainly less bruising. Dallas remembered this child having been beaten the night they'd come here and he looked up at her with a smile.

"I was trying to be careful. I swear I was."

Dallas nodded, not letting his smile falter.

"I don't want you to make me go back. Please don't make me go back. I won't let it happen again."

"Of course you won't. And I break stuff all the time." He picked her up and tried to ignore how stiff she became. "Let's make sure you're not cut then I'll clean this up. What's your name, little princess?"

"Luna. What's yours?"

Dallas sat her on the counter and reached for the first aid kit above her head. She was a cute little girl and looked like her mom, Georgia.

There was a small cut on her knee and another on her elbow. He washed them gently watching for any sign that he was hurting her. When she started to relax, he started making jokes that involved his brothers and sister.

"I'm Dallas Force. My sister Holly used to follow us around all the time when we were kids. She'd tell on us, too, when we did something wrong." He started to say how he'd gotten his bottom beat several times because of his sister, but let that part go. "We would get her later, though. When she was dating we'd tell when she kissed somebody. Have you kissed a boy yet?"

"No, sir. We aren't allowed to kiss nobody until the lord and master finds us a mate. Then we can only kiss him. It was almost my time when we left."

Everything in him froze as he looked at Stacy. The little girl couldn't have been right. She was barely old enough to be in school, certainly not someone's mate.

"We have to be ready no matter what or he beats us and makes us go anyway. Momma said that she would let me go over her body, but I don't know what that means. Do you?"

"It means she loves you very much." Dallas smiled, though he was sure that it didn't reach his eyes. "Luna, honey, why don't you go out and play for a bit. I want to help out in the kitchen for a change. I want to make a good impression on Stacy." He winked at her and she smiled.

She went out the door, taking the little boy that was watching the exchange between him and Luna carefully. He looked to be very protective of the girl and he wondered if someday he'd be calling to be her mate. It had been known to happen that way, children of a pack knowing almost from birth they were meant to be together. Dallas sat down in the chair and looked at Georgia, who'd been twisting a towel in her hands.

"I wouldn't have let him take her. Not without a fight. He said that he was getting into trouble because his numbers were too low. Lord Sterling said that it was our duty to—"

"You couldn't have stopped him and you know it. And he isn't a lord anything. He's a man, a dead wolf when I catch up to him." Georgia put her hands to her face and Dallas knew she was crying. Right now, he didn't have it in him to comfort her. He reached for his cell phone and called Austin. "We have to meet. Now. And make sure you let CJ know that I need to vent." He put down the phone and watched Stacy do what he couldn't. He looked up when she said his name.

"What are you going to do with Austin?"

"We're going to go on a run. A hard one. Will you be alright here?" She nodded. "I'm sorry, but I need—"

"Do not be. You need this. It is obvious that you need this. Go. I have things here. The children will be safe." He stood up and kissed her on the mouth. "Go now before I cannot let you."

Austin met him in the field between their houses. As they stripped down, Dallas told him what he'd found out. His brother was as shocked as he'd been. To give little girls, small children, to men for breeding…well, neither man would let that happen here.

"I've heard from the council. They want me to see what I can do about bringing him in alive."

Dallas snorted at his brother.

"I told them that I'd give it my best. Of course I didn't tell them that if he stepped on my land, he was as good as dead."

"So now what do we do? Oh by the way, I heard about your little fun at the man's house the other day. Next time you go out I would appreciate it if you'd let your enforcer know. Can't save your ass if I don't know where it's at." Austin nodded. "Also, what did you do with the money? I'm assuming the council doesn't know about that."

"Nope. But if I have to feed and shelter a bunch of new wolves, there has to be some extra capital involved. I've already talked to two of the contractors you set up appointments with. Thank you for that. They'll be starting on the houses and other outbuildings we need next week. I told both companies that the one that finishes first gets a bonus. I think I like having this much cash to use." Dallas asked how much. "Nearly twenty million. I had to count it twice before I believed it. What the hell was he doing with that much money and not caring for his people?"

Dallas didn't know, but he would bet that wasn't all of the money. If the man had that much there was no reason to believe that there hadn't been twice that much. "He wouldn't have left that bag of money in the driveway without a good reason. I'm betting he had carried all he could to the car by the time you guys pulled up."

He agreed. Then they shifted and took off. Dallas wanted to run hard and if they could bring down a deer for meat so much the better. Neither of them saw anything big enough to make it worth their while, but they needed this badly. When they finished and headed to the pack house Austin asked about Stacy.

"She's fine. I think she'd like to talk to you about her uncle. Not sure what you can do about his addiction, but she wants to try."

Austin nodded before answering. "Phil has an idea. He said that he can make the man think he doesn't want drugs any longer and then he thinks he can give him a fighting chance. He said, with your permission of course, that he'd like to try and boil the drugs out of his body."

"My permission? Why does he need mine?"

Austin shrugged.

"You tell him that. I'm not…wait. Could it have something to do with it being Stacy's uncle?"

"Don't know, but I can ask. But I wouldn't wait too long. Phil seems to think he'll die without the drugs or kill himself if we try to give him something to help him get off them." Austin stood on the porch. "You should also know that the uncle said he'd like to talk to Stacy when she wanted to come by, but for her to make it soon. Said he's not feeling well."

Austin went inside and Dallas started back to his home. He reached for Stacy and told her what he'd learned about Harvey. She sounded upset, but he didn't know her well enough yet to know why. But his wolf did stir and wanted to return to the house immediately to comfort her.

"I will see him tomorrow. I think I would like for it to be me alone. He might talk to me better without you or one of the others there."

Dallas thought she was right, but he didn't have to like it.

"I will be careful and not let him touch me. I know what the drug can do to a person."

CHAPTER 8

The news had nothing else to show but the burnt out shell of his house. Rich watched as each station showed the destruction and how it had been so far off the beaten path that, until someone called it in tonight, it would have gone undiscovered for who knew how long.

He looked around the house he'd stolen into and could smell the food cooking in the microwave. He didn't want the owners of the house to come home and catch him inside especially since, when he'd been looking for some clean clothes, he'd found all those guns.

He'd broken into the nice little house about an hour ago, right after he'd seen the owner and his little wife leave. He knew they were probably headed to their jobs by the briefcases and the large mugs of coffee in their hands.

Rich had come in the house by the locked back door and headed straight to the phone hanging on the wall. He'd been surprised by that too. A land line in a house this new? But calling the news station had been perfect. He'd reported the fire, wanted to know what was going to be done about it, and then had the audacity to ask them if there was a reward. He might have gotten it too if he could have had an address and been able to give them the phone number he'd been calling from. But he knew neither and hung up.

The microwave dinged in the kitchen and he left the big screen in the living room in favor of the littler one in the kitchen. He pulled his still hot food from the machine then sat at the table with a bottle of wine he'd found in the refrigerator, as well as the leftovers he was now enjoying. There was a whole apple pie in there he was planning to have as well. The news anchor was still talking about the shame of it all.

"There seems to be no one living here, Michelle. We've had crews looking around for someone, anyone who can say who the family was that lived here, but there doesn't seem to be anyone around." The camera panned to the once beautiful building. "The only thing we can think is they have been on vacation. A Mr. Richard O'Brien and his family have lived in the home for more than twenty years, but according to records they all died some years back."

"That'll be a horrific thing to come home to no matter who it is. To have lost everything without knowing until you got back. My heart goes out to them." The woman in the newsroom then turned from the television where Adie Pinkersmith was at his house to the camera in front of her. "If anyone knows the whereabouts of this family, please contact your local police department."

He was just cutting into the pie when he heard the door in the front open. He nearly swallowed the spoon he'd been using to scoop the ice cream into his bowl. The woman who came into the kitchen wasn't the one he saw leaving and, when she screamed, he tossed both the pie and the ice cream container at her. He knew he'd hit her, but not how badly because he'd taken off out the back door as fast as he could go. He was nearly down the street when he realized he'd left his things in the house. He actually thought about going back and getting his dirty clothes and the cell phone he'd found in the house, but decided that, the way she'd screamed, there would be a good possibility that the cops were already there.

"Damn, damn, damn," he cursed as soon as he stopped running. He'd been so winded by the time he'd gotten to the outskirts of town that he thought maybe the dinner or the ice cream had been tainted. He couldn't believe how short of a distance he could go before he'd feel like the needed a nap. Rich sat near the tree he'd been leaning against.

He looked down at his body. When he'd broken into the house today he'd been surprised how tightly the man's clothes fit him. It had been so bad that he'd had to go and find something a lot looser to wear. He'd finally ended up in a pair of sleep pants and a really baggy sweatshirt.

Rich realized that he'd put on some weight. He'd believed that it hadn't been all that much and told himself that when it got to be a problem he'd do something about it. Well, he'd waited too long. He was a fat blob.

And he knew it wasn't just vanity talking either. When he'd gotten out of the shower and stepped on the scale, it had said he was close to three hundred-fifty pounds. Nearly three times what he'd weighed when he'd become pack leader at only one-twenty. For reason's he couldn't imagine were right he blamed this on this nemesis too. He was fat because of Austin Force.

In the back of his mind he knew that wasn't possible. He'd not even known the man for all that long, had never actually met him, but he had to blame someone and he was simply the best possible source. Rich lay down next to the tree and closed his eyes. He couldn't even look at himself. It was time to make it an issue and lose the weight. But first, he was going to kill that bastard.

Moving slowly, he made his way back to the cave. It was the best possible place for him to be right now. He was exhausted, hungry again, and had to plan. He knew where the other pack was and all he needed to do was find a way onto the property, kill the bastard, then wait for them to fall apart before he stepped in as new pack leader. He was laughing to himself as he entered the cave. In a week's time he'd not only have Georgia and her brats back, who he only just realized he was going to kill as soon as he got them, but he'd have a new pack, a better home, and maybe a new bitch to call his own. Life was going to get a great deal better.

He was only about five miles from the pack where he was currently. That meant that once he got the wolf and killed him he'd be able to get back here to hide until they did what he expected them to.

But what if he was injured? It was a good possibility with him being so out of shape, so he had to think that through as well. He should have a backup plan. What if he simply lured the wolf here and then killed him? That would work.

But drugging the wolf would be better. Then he could bring him back here, tie him up, and make him pay for all the things he'd made Rich suffer through. He had a long list too.

Okay, he thought, and started to make a list in the dirt. Drugs. He'd have to find something that would knock him out completely without killing him. Rich liked the idea of bringing him to heel and, the more he thought about it, the better he liked it. He thought about some of the drugs he'd taken recently and decided that he'd be better off getting something that didn't enhance his abilities and only put him down. At least for a little while.

He started making a longer list and pulled open the bag of chips he'd snatched the day before. He wasn't fond of chips really, but they took away the hunger pangs. Tomorrow he was going to use some of the money he'd stashed in the hidey hole he'd had and buy him something to eat, to wear, and also maybe a map or at least some paper to use.

Smiling, as he closed his eyes he thought about the transgressions list he'd made. The wolf was going to be lucky if he made it after the first hour. Rich fell asleep after finishing off the chips and starting on the second bag. He wanted to get going as soon as light crested over the mountain.

~~~

Phil looked down at the man he'd turned vampire. Well, he and Holly had changed. Phil genuinely liked Myles and hadn't wanted him to die a senseless death. Changing him had been the only thing he'd been able to do to make it so his friend would be around a bit longer.

"You can do this. All you have to do is make him believe what it is that you want him to and it will work."

Myles looked at him before looking at the cell door again.

"Just go in and do it. I'll be right there with you so, if you don't do something right, I can drain you both." He'd meant it as a joke, but Myles was either too tense to recognize it or he'd really been reading up on what he could do. Phil laughed when Myles had brought him the smut book he'd given him the week after he'd been changed.

"This is really…well, I didn't think you get books like this in print. I thought…I don't know, I guess it was more of a woman's kind of read. You said she was a vampire? Is she dating anyone?" There had been laughter, but Phil thought the new vamp had been serious.

"No, not that I know of. But she's one of the ancient ones. I guess she'd be nearly my mom's age, maybe a little older." The author he'd told him to read was also a friend of his. Phil thought maybe in a few years he'd introduce the former cop to her. She was something of an enigma to even him.

His voice brought him to the present. "I just use that weird voice and he'll do what I need for him to do. Seems simple enough. What are the side effects?"

"It's called compulsion, and side effects? Let me see… None if you do it right. Insanity if you don't. But I'm right here so you'll do fine." Phil waited a few heart beats. "Have you tried biting anyone yet?"

"No," Myles practically screamed at him. Then in a much calmer voice, "No. I'm not…you said I'd be fine until I was ready. And I'm not. Ready, I mean. I want to be sure that…I can't do it yet. Especially to a man. I've been…I can't. Not yet."

Phil nodded. He understood. He remembered his first time and smiled. But he'd been prepared for it. This man had been dropped into it. He nodded to the door. "We need to do this, Myles. The man needs to be dried out." He walked to the door. "Stacy wants him around and this will be the only way."

They walked into the small cell and looked at the pitiful wolf sitting in the corner curled into a ball. He was muttering to himself and Phil knew that he'd reached the point that if he didn't get dried out or get drugs soon he'd take his own life. He was already shaking and had lost weight in the few days he'd been here. Phil said his name and Harvey looked up at him.

"Do you have something to ease the memories with you? Stacy said she'd take care of me. I don't want to remember this anymore." He put his head on his drawn up knees. "I don't want to remember what he did. Please let me…give me something, I beg you."

"We're going to give you something. Something that will make you feel much better." Phil nodded at Myles. "I have a friend here I'd like for you to meet. He's going to give you what you need."

"Harvey, my name is Kramer, Myles Kramer. I'm here to help you."

Harvey looked at him though bloodshot eyes then back to the floor in front of him.

"You'll need to look at me for me to help you."

"I'd rather just die, thank you, though. I've been…I let him kill them both and I did nothing to help them because I was a fool." He glanced up before looking back down. "Just do me a favor and kill me now. I know what you are and my blood, while tainted, is better than a drug." He laughed bitterly, but didn't look up.

Phil put his hand on Myles' shoulder and pushed him to the floor. *"Pull his chin up and he'll look at you. As soon as he makes eye contact you'll have to work fast to make him continue to look at you."* He reached Myles through their link and continued to encourage him. *"As soon as you have his mind tell him that he'll not want drugs again. That as soon as he thinks about them he'll get ill and not want anything to do with them. Then, once you do that, I'll fix his body."*

Phil watched as Myles did what he'd told him to do. It was practice for him really. It was a way to get used to some of the powers that he had and to use them under circumstances that Phil, as his maker, could control. What Phil had planned was much more dangerous and a whole lot more work. He was glad that he'd fed well before coming here to do this.

As soon as Harvey nodded that he'd understood Myles and that as far as he was concerned there would be no more drugs passing through his body, Phil knelt down in from of the man as Myles stood up.

He took the man's arm and pulled up his torn sleeve. Track marks nearly the length of his arm were red and bruised. He could see his legs were as bad. Phil could make those go away too, the reminders that he'd been a drug addict for a long time, but didn't want the man to be too terrified about all this.

Phil ran his sharpened nail down the needle marks and watched the small drops of blood gather there. It wasn't to bleed him out, but to have an outlet for the poison that was there. Phil closed his eyes and used his magic to make the nasty shit the man had been putting in his veins for so long leave.

He heard the man sobbing. He had expected that. Men or women doing drugs this long would feel the withdrawal much more than a new junkie. Even the begging, begging to be left alone was expected. What he'd not expected was the connection he'd gotten from the man, the almost maker to child kind of connection. And he'd learned a great deal more about Harvey's brother.

When Phil fell back against the floor exhausted, he reached for his mate. *"Come to me now. I need for you to relay a message to your brother."*

Holly was there almost instantly. One of the things she'd gotten from him was his ability to travel quickly on her own. He took her hand into his and gave her what he could, nearly everything that he'd gotten from the man, excluding the drugs.

"Tell your brother to go there now. There is more money there than he could spend in several lifetimes." He pulled his hand free, but nearly wept with relief when he smelled her blood at his nose. "I love you."

"I love you too, you moron. Now feed. And if you think this gets you out of getting yelled at later then you're nuttier than the man in the corner."

He drank from her greedily and felt his cock swell.

"Behave. We have company and I don't have time for your shenanigans right now."

He could smell her need and was pretty sure that both men could as well. A low growl made Myles leave the room, but Harvey could not. He looked up at her as he sealed the tiny wounds. "I'll expect you back later. I have a need to make you mine again." He sent her thoughts and visuals of just what he planned to do to her. "And that's not even half of it."

She left him there to go to her brother after a long and very unsatisfying kiss from her. He looked over at Harvey. What to do with him now, he wondered. He was pretty sure that he'd not reach for his brother the alpha, but wasn't sure if the idiot could reach for Harvey. He decided to leave him here for now but make things a bit more comfortable for him. He was very glad that Myles had also forbidden him to kill himself or harm himself in any way. Phil was proud of the man for thinking of it.

CHAPTER 9

Dallas went to the area and looked around. It was pretty much as Holly had told him it would be, but nothing too out of place. The large dead tree was just where he'd been told and he went there to see if the thing was as full as he'd been told it would be.

It was.

The bags, back packs, briefcases, as well as trash bags were all there. He pulled them out and set them on the ground beside him. He heard the Jeep pull up and only stopped long enough to see that it was his mate before he pulled out the last four bags.

"That's all the money?"

He shrugged before picking up the first bag and opening it.

"Holy shit. What the fuck was he doing saving it if he didn't use it for his pack? How much would you guess is there?"

Dallas didn't know, but he'd bet his last nickel it was more than even Harvey had thought. He tossed the bags in the back of the Jeep and pulled her into his arms. He'd not seen her much today and needed her badly. "I want you to get naked and lay down. I want to eat you. I didn't get to last night and I so want to play." She grinned at him, but didn't

KATHI S. BARTON

move. "Or I can strip you down to your skin and have you standing up."

She still didn't move and he took a step with her to back her against the car. When he reached out to take her shirt into his hands he watched her eyes darken with need. Tearing her shirt from her, he heard her sigh. When she reached up, unclasped her bra, began to cup her own breasts and play with her nipples, he dropped down in front of her.

The jeans didn't fare any better than her shirt. But he had her, now, where he wanted her. Putting his hands into the sides of her panties and pulling them from her, he watched her breasts tighten.

"Please, Dallas. I want to feel your tongue inside of me. Please?" She opened her legs and leaned back against the Jeep. "Please?"

He kissed her mound and then licked the clit that was peeking out from her tender folds. When she moaned low he teased her with his tongue before taking the little nubbin into his mouth and suckling.

Wet heat filled his mouth and he needed more. Lifting her leg up and resting it on his shoulder, he opened her wider for him. Now he could take her harder, deeper into his mouth.

Her first climax was a surprise. When she cried out she wound her fingers into his hair and held him to her as she flooded his mouth. Sliding his finger into her sheath, he felt her tighten around him and, before he could go much further, she came again. As he laid her down she was begging him to take her.

"Not yet," he said to her as he guided her to the ground. "I need my fun. You've come so fast that I've gotten a good taste, but I want the climax that you've been holding back from me."

"Holding back? Are you nuts? I've come so hard that I don't think I can move after that." He moved between her legs and settled in. "Dallas, please? I want you to fuck me. Please?"

"Not yet. And you do have one. I promise you. When you come you'll see what I mean." He slid his fingers inside of her and watched her eyes close. "Watch me, love. I want to look up and see your eyes when you're ready for me."

He wanted to take her now. He wanted, not just to fuck her, but to pound into her deep, fill her with his cock and then his seed. Moving slowly to her pussy he marveled again that she was finally his.

When he took her juices into him this time he let a little of his beast go. Not enough to shift, but enough that his wolf could taste her. He felt his tongue lengthen and stretch so that she could feed him.

His wolf stirred then growled low his satisfaction at the treat he was getting. Dallas reached down and unsnapped his pants to free his painful cock and drank more from her. He watched her face, looking for the moment she was at her peak again.

"Dallas, Dallas, Dallas, Dallas, Dallas, Dallas," she said his name over and over. When he felt her getting close he sat up and nearly went back to dining on the best meal he'd ever had when she whimpered.

His clothes were off and he was settled at her entrance. Dallas slid in slowly; his cock filled her and his wolf snarled at him. He was going to have her faint from this encounter and, when she did, he was going to crow like a fool.

Her legs wrapped around him and her body rose up to meet him, trying to encourage him to deepen himself into her. But he only stopped. When she whimpered again and laid back, he moved slowly into her. In and out, he took his time.

He wanted this to last, and it would even if it nearly killed him.

When he was as far as he could go, his balls at her warm, wet ass, he started to roll into her, looking for the moment when he touched her sweet spot. Every time he touched it, she tightened. When she did, he'd purposely miss it a few times until she was under control again. Dallas felt the sweat roll off his back.

His cock was full and he could feel his balls tighten against his body. He was so ready that he knew if he waited much longer he was going to hurt when he did finally come. When he nuzzled her neck, finding the pulse beating hard enough to nearly hear, he touched her inside once then a second time. She was tightening around him so much now that he was having trouble fucking her around it.

His cock lurched in her. Knowing that he'd reached even his limits he surged again. This time he felt her come; her entire body tensed for several seconds before she started to scream. Dallas bit her, sank his canines deep and then bit harder still. Her strangled scream this time told him what his body already knew.

She was his.

Their climax went on. And when she bit him in the shoulder he held his teeth into her flesh. His own body was trying to give her its all and he nearly blacked out twice when she screamed again. After her body and his settled he released her throat. Then licked the blood clean and sealed the wound. There was a mark there this time, a scar already forming so that anyone looking at her would know she belonged to someone, belonged to him. He lifted his eyes to hers and looked down at her sleeping form.

Blood still stained her own mouth. Her lips were swollen from biting him. Dallas couldn't help but stare at her, knowing that for as long as they lived this memory, this picture of her in his mind, would be the one that stayed with him through death. He kissed her gently on the mouth and left her body.

Standing up, Dallas walked to the Jeep. There were clothes there, a bag that was now in each car they had, as well as hidden in a few places in the forest. And there, on the seat was a set of clothes for Stacy. He grinned when he looked back at her. She'd planned to seduce him, the little vixen. Dressing quickly, he picked her up and put her in the back seat. She didn't even stir. Getting into the Jeep he found himself whistling all the way back to his house. Dallas was in love and didn't care who knew it.

~~~

Connor looked over the bags lying on the floor, then at the money stacked up on the table. Well, in this case, tables. He'd never seen so much money that wasn't directly attached to a drug bust. He decided he should say something, but for the life of him couldn't think what it would be but, "*wow*."

"What do you think he did to get so much of this? I mean, there is over ninety million dollars here. Even if he collected monies annually like Georgia said, that's a shit ton of money to amass over twenty years." Myles picked up a stack of fifties. "She said they had to pay an annual fee of what? Half their income? What the hell were these people doing that paid so fucking well?"

"There were a lot more of them when the pack was with his predecessor." Stacy moved in the room slowly and with grace, as she did everything, he'd noticed. Then he saw her scar, looked to his brother, and smiled as she continued. "The pack was huge, nearly ten thousand strong. Then over the years the numbers began to…lower. I think now it had more to do with deaths than people moving on."

"We've come across several more mass graves. All of them with the driver's licenses in a steel box and when they were young, too young to do more than be a body count, there were certificates of birth." Myles nodded toward several large boxes grimly. "Most of those we have found over the past few days and, according to your uncle, there are a great many more. Do you think Sterling knows about that money? Do you think it's possible that Harvey put it there in hopes of getting away on his own?"

Connor shook his head at Myles' questions.

"Then why save it that way? Why not...I don't know, bank it?"

"My uncle said that he and his mate had decided to leave earlier the morning she was murdered. He said that he had made the mistake of going to my father and telling him that they were not happy and that they would like to go out to find another pack, maybe become the alpha after a few years." She reached for Dallas' hand and held it as she continued. "He told me that he had been assigned another duty, this one that took him out to the far reaches of the territory. He would be gone for two days. Before he had gotten halfway to the place he was to be he felt his mate's cry. By the time he had gotten back it was too late."

"So your father killed his own brother's mate and child." Austin stood up to pace. He'd been so quiet all morning that Connor had forgotten he was even there. "Then what, he started to give him drugs to make him do all the dirty work that his alpha needed?"

It wasn't a question, but Stacy answered anyway. "Yes. He said that he had started off giving him something to sleep. Then something more to keep him awake during the day. Uncle Harvey said that by then he had not cared. He wanted to forget." Stacy looked at Dallas, and Connor knew that whatever was said next wasn't easy for the girl. "My father had him dispose, that is what he called it *dispose,* of his own wife and unborn child. He told me that he'd never felt such anguish. His daughter had died in the womb, but his wife had not been dead when he'd made it back to his home. She died in his arms, loving him for being there for her. I believe that alone has made him what he is."

"Mother fuck," Austin exploded, then took several deep breaths. When his wolf started to surface, all of them felt him. It was a powerful emotion to bring a wolf to front for an alpha. "Stacy, do you know if Harvey remembers where she's buried?"

"Yes. She and his daughter are not in the mass graves as my father thinks, but in one that he dug on his own. He said that they are on your property and that he visits them when he can." She looked up at Austin. "You will not move them, will you, alpha? That is all that keeps him from joining them, knowing that they are close and not with the others."

"Of course not. And as soon as this mess is over, we'll erect a marker in their honor. But we have to take care of this man. Do we have any idea where he is? I thought by now he would have taken the bait and come here for what he considers his property." Stacy didn't answer and no one else knew either.

"What about all of this? I'm honestly not sure how I feel about this. The money belongs to the pack and the pack is now yours. I'm sure that's how it works, right?" All of them nodded at Myles' question. "Then I guess our next question should be, how do you use it?"

"Buildings first and foremost. I have some construction companies working on that now. And I've just been informed that a large section of land to the south of us came to the pack this morning." Austin looked pointedly at Stacy. "It seems that someone donated it as a member of the pack."

"It belonged to me to use as I saw fit. I do not have to explain myself to you. Should you not want it then I am sure that there are any number of packs or businesses that would—"

"Simmer down. I was kidding you. Yes, I want it...we want it. There are several hundred acres there that we can use." Austin kissed Stacy's cheek then frowned at Dallas when he growled. "Sorry. I was only happy is all. Anyway—"

The phone ringing startled them all. His mom walked into the room and reached for it just as it rang a second time. She was smiling when she answered and it suddenly turned to a frown. She looked at him when she handed him the phone.

"The house and building are gone, Mrs. Force. All of it." Connor couldn't understand what was going on, but he did recognize the voice, one of the officers that he'd worked for with the police. "Been trying to contact Connor all morning and he ain't answering his phone. His house is a'burning right now."

Connor calmed the man then hung up a few minutes later. He looked at his family. "My house is gone. Someone set it to flames about an hour ago, it seems, and then most of the studio went up as well."

"Ah, Connor, I'm so sorry." Austin pulled him into a hug, but all he felt was numbness. Everything he had, owned, and things he'd never replace, were gone.

He looked at his family. "What am I supposed to do now?" No one answered because they didn't know either. "I'm homeless. I didn't much care for my house, but the things in it? Things that were Dad's and our grandparents' are all gone." He moved to the yard to go home, to see what was there or not there, and was nearly in the car when he felt someone pushing him to the passenger's side. His family piled into the big SUV and helped him buckle. All he wanted to do was go alone, but was suddenly glad they were going too.

It was a mess. The fire department had done a good job of keeping it out of the forest surrounding his home, but it had been a total loss on his house. The studio, where he made molds for things and did some art when he had time, was mostly destroyed, but the back and the basement were still there. Very little, however, escaped the smoke damage and water. He stood back and watched as the last wall in his home fell.

Connor was staring at Phil before he realized the man was there. He knew the man was speaking, but wasn't entirely sure what he was saying until he shook him. Connor bit his tongue he'd been rattled so hard. Phil finally got through to him.

"I said this is what I could get. I reported the fire, but there was no way that I could save it all." Connor looked at the pile of things lying on the ground. "I'm just glad that last week you showed me those things or I wouldn't have had a clue what to grab first."

Connor dropped to the ground and touched the things lying there. His pictures in the large boxes that he'd been meaning to hang and sort. There was his father's rifle, the one that he'd shown Connor how to shoot when he'd turned thirteen. A shirt that had been his grandda's that lay on the back of the couch, a cookbook that his grandmother had given him when he'd moved into the house. Connor stood up and grabbed the big vamp.

"You couldn't have…I don't know…you've no idea what you've done for me. It's all here. All of the treasures that I have… Oh Phil, I can't begin to tell you what this means to me."

Phil nodded and pulled away. The man was either going to have to get used to hugs or he was forever going to be uncomfortable. As soon as he was within reach of the others, each of them grabbed him up and pulled him to their bodies. By the time he'd made the rounds the poor man was flustered and out of sorts. Funny, but Connor had a feeling that the man probably loved it as much as he complained about it.

The house was finally out. The fire hadn't burned long because it wasn't really all that big, one bedroom, kitchen, living room, great room, and a bath. And it was made of logs. Connor listened as the fire marshal told his attorney, Phil it just so happened, that the fire was set and that, pending an investigation, he was willing to bet it came back as gasoline was used as the accelerant.

"I know you weren't involved. Been in this business long enough to know when a man has lost it all. Besides, you were just telling me how much you put into it this summer when the storms came a'busting through. New roof and all, I'd say you had more invested in the house than you'll get from insurance. Unless, of course, you had one of them riders on it."

"He did. All the houses that I help with do. I make sure they have them." Phil winked at him. "Thanks, Roger. I'll make sure I get the claim in as soon as you close on this and I'll make sure I tell the mayor what a great job you and your boys did to keep this under control. Fire like this could have been a lot nastier if it had gotten away."

Connor didn't care, nor did he understand what the men were talking about. A rider? No clue. He was simply happy that he had some of his things left.

CHAPTER 10

Rich was laughing so hard he nearly missed where he'd been staying. The cave looked much like all the others in the area and he'd been distracted. He'd finally had some payback.

The only thing he regretted were the burns on his arms. The stupid fire had gotten away from him and he'd nearly not made it out of the house alive. But he'd made the bastard pay. Much better than he'd ever dreamed he would.

He'd seen the man coming out of the house earlier that morning. It had only taken him a little while to figure out it was the same man that had been at his own home only days before. The bastard Austin Force. There, of course, had been some slight differences, too small to quibble over, but he knew it was him. Now all he had to do was wait, wait and see how the man reacted to such news.

Rich looked down at the burns that hadn't healed when he'd shifted. They should have, but now they were sorer than before. He wondered if the man had planted a trap in his house in the event that he tried to burn it down. He wouldn't put it past him. He peered harder at them and saw that they were sort of seeping and looked bad. He smelled them and all he could detect was soot and burning flesh. At times like these he wished for his brother.

He'd been trying to contact Harvey every day and still nothing. He didn't think he was dead, but he also didn't think he was strong enough to go without the drugs for as long as he had. Unless, of course, he was getting them from someone else, which would be surprising as Harvey rarely left the compound and, when he did, it was only because Rich had made him.

But for now he was content to think his brother had been hurt badly in some sort of an accident and that was why he'd not been answering him. No, the only reason that came to mind was that he was going through detoxification somewhere and that was why he was unable to reach him. Harvey had a lot to answer for. But Rich was willing to cut him some slack if he returned soon and helped him gather his fold. But then he was as dead as the rest.

Rich cleaned himself up in the pond that he'd come across earlier that day. He needed to go into town this evening and get a few things. One of which was a place to stay. He was tired of staying in the cave and wanted some of the luxuries that he'd had to give up when…well, when Austin came to bother him.

He'd come to the realization that Georgia Reynolds had been having an affair with Force all along. That was why she'd so readily gone with him and now stayed with him. And Force had her in some sort of compulsion mind hold. She no more wanted to stay with Force than she'd wanted to leave Rich's pack. That's the reason she'd left, not anything at all to do with her mate being killed.

Rich tried to think how her mate had been killed. There had been a mix-up at one point, but he had no idea what it had been about. Tim, he remembered now, had been with him and he remembered there had been blood. But not a great deal, but… Rich rubbed his forehead and tried to think. But the harder he tried, the more it hurt.

After an hour of lying down, he started into town. He had only a little money, not the sum of money he'd had, though. Again, he had a hard time trying to think where he'd used it. Harvey usually took care of these things and now he was being an ass and Rich didn't have his help to keep track. He walked the nearly two miles in what he thought was record time at four hours. Rich went into the first shop he came to.

"Burnt it to the ground, they said. Nearly had that lawyer of theirs burned up too. Worst thing in history here since…well, can't remember when."

Rich looked over at the two men standing at the counter and tried to listen to what they were saying as well as find some of the items on his list.

"You remember a few years back there, Tom, when that little kid, what was his name, burned that shed up that belonged to the lady on that road at the other end of town?" Rich stared at the two men and, when the other nodded, Rich tried to decipher what had been said. "Well, that was bad too, but all that got burned up then was a few hoes and a lawnmower that probably hadn't started since her kid lit out for greener pastures."

Rich moved away from them. It was that or he was going to have to have them explain what they were talking about and he'd been trying hard not to make himself known. He could see that there was a diner of sorts in the back, so he went there. Three televisions were blaring some game on them while the one right behind the bar had the news on. And, oh wow, it was about the Force household.

"…earlier this morning and, now that the fire crew is gone, you can see what a devastation it is. Connor Force has been on the police department for nearly five years and has recently, along with his brother and another retired police officer, opened their own agency. Mr. Force, along with his family, had this to say about the fire and his loss."

"I want to thank all those who came out to help the fire department. It was nice to see the community gather together in times of need. I don't know who would set such a fire, but I'm very glad that I was able to save some of my more precious memories by having them in the car instead of the house." He looked right at the camera as he continued. *"I hope that the person who did this is aware of what happens to people who burn other people's property."*

Rich looked around, sure that this Force was right here with him. He wasn't just a little afraid, but terrified that the male had full knowledge as to who had burned him out. And worst yet, he'd gotten the wrong Force to boot.

Connor Force, not Austin, and a cop too. Now what? Rich moved out of the little diner, suddenly very afraid. He nearly yelped when someone dropped something on the floor beside him. He moved out of the shop completely and was nearly down the street when he realized that he still needed a place to stay. Turning to the first little house he saw, he walked up to the door and opened it.

He decided that he'd either have a place to stay in this house, which he found highly unlikely, or he'd simply make it his house to stay in. Either way, he had a hidey hole. As soon as the elderly woman came from the kitchen drying her hands Rich decided that he didn't want to negotiate and reached out to her and snapped her neck. A check of the rest of the house showed that he was alone. There was no one else in the house but a big tom cat which, once he showed it what he was, took off like its tail was on fire.

He turned on the television after taking her body to the basement and stuffing her into the chest freezer. Of course he made sure that he'd taken all the food out of it first and brought it up the stairs to stash in the smaller freezer. The woman fit nicely and he was thawing out three steaks as he tried to figure out the remote on the television. She didn't even have cable. And the local news was still going on and on about the game he'd seen at the diner, as well as small snippets of the fire.

After frying up the steaks and baking four potatoes in the microwave he settled into the big recliner in the living room. As he drifted off he smiled. Tomorrow he'd go back to the house he'd burned and see if he could find more information about Austin. Then he'd kill this Connor person as well.

~~~

Dallas watched as Phil was being grilled by Austin. He thought if he asked the vampire once more if he was sure who had burned the house down he might attack him too. Phil leaned back in his chair and smiled.

"You ask me if I'm sure again and I will give you details about the sex your sister and I had right before I came here. I can go into so many details that—"

"No. Damn it. I just want to be sure. If I go to the council and tell them that I think it was him then they will only tell me to bide my time. I want this prick gone before he hurts someone else." Austin sat down finally. "You have no idea how badly I feel because Connor lost his house. I taunted the man and now this. This is entirely my fault."

"No, it wasn't. Not entirely. The man would have come to you sooner or later. He had to know that you were the men standing there that morning and now he can't find his brother, and his pack, what little there was of it, is gone as well." Dallas got up to get a few beers as he continued. "Besides, if you hadn't gone there and gotten his money these people would be still suffering and, worse yet, no telling how many more of them would be dead."

They drank in quiet. Dallas looked over at Phil and smiled. "Would you have really given details of your sex life to him if he hadn't shut up?" Phil nodded then shook his head. "I thought so. Holly would have staked you."

"Probably. She can be a bit...violent when the mood strikes her." Phil laughed. "What about you and Stacy? Any plans for the future yet?"

"We're still getting to that. You do remember that I have about two hundred people in my house right now, don't you? We've not even been able to...the bed is being used for sleeping and not much more." Phil laughed and Dallas grinned. "Laugh it up, mosquito. Some of us don't have the luxury of having a house as big as a hotel."

"Hey, I offered. But it seems they're a mite skittish of sleeping in a house with a vampire. I tried to tell them that I wouldn't feed from them, but no one was willing to try. I'll have to win them over with my charm, I suppose."

Dallas rolled his eyes and looked up at Austin when he cleared his throat.

"If you two are done bonding I'd like to get back to the issue we have here." Austin sat down again. Dallas wondered if he realized how much he'd been pacing over the past several days. "We have enough money here for several packs. I'm not saying we won't use some of it to build and to make us a better pack, but I think I'd like to set up some of the money so that it'll go back to the families that have come from him. Sort of a trust fund or something."

Phil nodded. "I can set that up for you. You might want to keep some of it back and use it for educational purposes too. College is expensive and you could run a scholarship program for all the pack."

The phone ringing had them looking at each other then at the phone again. So far, lately, there had not been a great deal of good news coming from the thing. Austin got up to answer it and Dallas knew immediately who had called.

"Yes, this is Austin Force." A pause and then a bark of laughter. "Yes, Sterling, I have your pack and a damn fine one it is too."

Phil got up, looked at the caller ID, and wrote down the number. When he handed it to Dallas he nearly burst out laughing. The idiot was calling from the local grocery store that he'd programmed into the phone only yesterday for his mom to get supplies she'd needed.

"I'll be back. I have to—" A hand on his shoulder from Austin kept Phil from leaving.

"No, Sterling, I'm not afraid of you, but if you harm one more person, human or anyone else, I will be the one hunting and you'll be the one that's dead. And know this, a trial will be the least of your problems." Austin hung up and stood there for several seconds. Neither he nor Phil said a word until Austin went to the refrigerator, took out another bottle of beer, and sat down.

"I could have gone there and taken him out. No one would have been the wiser about it." Phil looked over at him when Austin didn't speak. "What's up with him?"

"He has two of my pack, he said. And since I don't know if he means mine or his, I can't reach out to them."

Dallas was afraid for his mate and reached for her.

"I am fine. I have something to tell you, but not this way. Where are you now?" He told her. *"I will arrive shortly. There has been another killing, but not one of us this time. A human woman entered a house she was to clean and a man fitting my father's description ran out the back. She was only able to tell the police what he looked like before dying from a*

knife to the chest. It looks as if he was having a meal and has stolen clothes. He left his prints as well as his clothing behind for evidence."

Dallas told his brother and Phil. "It sounds as if he's getting sloppy. Not that he has given much indication that he was overly smart anyway, but leaving DNA as well as prints everywhere means he's not thinking."

Austin nodded and Phil stood. "I'm going to the house where the woman was killed. Maybe I can find out something more than they have knowledge of. And before you ask, I will only go to the store if I'm sure he's gone. I want him dead, but if he has people hidden away I want to find them as badly as you do."

He was suddenly gone. Dallas looked at his brother and knew the man was suffering. This was overwhelming to him and he wasn't as much in charge as Austin. When he spoke Dallas knew that he was nearing his end at dealing with this in the proper channels.

"I want more patrol around the houses as well as the perimeter. This man has gone from being an irritant to being an all-out pain in my ass." Dallas pulled out the small notebook he always had and began writing things down. "Double up on the houses that we've got the other pack in and bring in another doctor. I heard from CJ that a few of the families not used to having meat are sick. Also, see what you can do about getting someone here that can evaluate where the children are educationally."

Dallas looked up. "Education? Shouldn't we be worried more on housing and getting this prick taken care of than what grade little Sally should be in?"

He flushed when Austin looked at him angrily. But Austin didn't yell at him, simply took a deep breath before answering.

"*I* need this. I need something I can control right now and education seems the easiest to take care of. I need to do something that feels like I'm making a difference in their lives and not keeping them in homes with people they don't know eating food they aren't familiar with and getting sick." Austin looked out the window. "A few of the children are staying at our home. One of the little boys was terrified of me when I raised my voice to the television when I was watching a game the other night."

"They're terrified of me too. Stacy said they aren't used to having big men be kind to them. I'm sorry, Austin. I'll do whatever you need for me to do." Austin nodded. "What are we going to do with all this money? We can't simply not tell anyone about it. Someone is going to start asking questions when we pay cash for things we couldn't before."

"Phil said he had that under control. Something about a long lost relative leaving us with a great deal of money. Since there are six of us, including mom, we can bring in a great deal and only have to pay inheritance tax on it. I'm not sure of the details, but he said it would work." Austin looked around the room. "We have to make this work, Dallas. This is what we wanted since we moved here and started our own pack."

Dallas nodded. He was right, they did want to grow, but he doubted that either of them thought it would be like this. Thinking back he'd thought of maybe a couple hundred wolves or less. As it was, right now they had over three hundred and growing. He grinned when he looked at Austin again.

"Did you know that Holly was whelping?"

Austin went from overwhelmed-looking to pissed in a heartbeat.

"Yeah, I heard it from Connor a couple of days ago. Phil hasn't even told his family yet."

As soon as the vampire came back into the house Austin hit him. Phil didn't move off the floor, but looked up at him. He seemed to know why he'd been hit.

"I thought you knew about the birds and the bees, big guy. You do have kids of your own. Maybe I should have a talk—"

"Get up so I can knock you down again." Austin clenched his fists twice and looked ready to drag the vampire up. "I mean it. I need a good beating and you're just the—ouch. What the hell was—"

"Don't make me have to hit you again. I don't care how big you think you are; you do not hit a man because you feel he's done something wrong." Their mom stood behind her son tapping her foot and holding her wooden spoon like she was ready to use it on him again. "Austin Jackson Force, you help that man up right now before I really get mad."

"He knocked up Holly. What the he...heck am I supposed to do?" Austin helped Phil up a little too much and he nearly fell again. A glare from their mom had Austin moving back rather than letting him fall.

"You should congratulate him, not kill him. Phil, would you please accept my profound apologizes? I did raise him better than this."

Phil kissed her on the cheek. "No harm done. None at all. Holly might be a tad upset, but not me. I'm excited." Phil was still grinning when he sat down and looked at both of them before he told them what he'd figured out. "The man smells like death. He's killed someone else by his own hand, but I could not smell another wolf around where he'd been at the pay phone."

"A human?"

Phil nodded at Dallas' question.

"He's probably taken someone's house over and decided that rather than take the chance of being caught again, he'd simply take out the middle man and live there."

Stacy entering the house made him growl low. She smelled of wolf and not him. She came and sat on his lap without being asked and laid her head on his shoulder. He looked at his mother when she shooed everyone out of the room.

"My father has killed so many. I do not want to bring this on your head, but I think I should leave." He lifted her chin up so that he could look into her eyes. "I have brought shame to your family."

Dallas lifted her into his arms and stood. He needed her more at this moment than any other time. Carrying her out into the night, he held her all the way to their house and took her to their room. He was going to make his mate need him as much as he needed her.

CHAPTER 11

Stacy followed the path her uncle had told her about. She'd not been there for many years and didn't want to get lost on his property. It was the place she'd been told her mother and she had lived before her father had murdered her.

"It's a small place she had. It was mine, see, and I wanted her to have something nice. Rich had nothing and was more than willing to take something for nothing from another wolf. He always acted as if he was supposed to get more than anyone else's share." She watched him stretch and noticed how much thinner he was, but his color was better.

"You let them live on your property? I did not know you had any." She flushed when he smiled at her. "I am sorry. You were not a pauper when you came to this pack, I know."

He took her hand and she held on. The table they were sitting at, in addition to the rest of the nicer furniture, made the larger cell look homier rather than prisonlike. He'd been told that he was safest in there rather than in a house where Rich could contact him.

"Did you ever wonder why you spoke so well? Never using contractions and speaking so softly?"

She shook her head.

"Your mother wanted you to be well thought of. She wanted only the best for you and when I found you a home to hide you away I looked for one that would give you the best education."

She looked away from him, not wanting him to know that the man and woman she'd been with had beaten the way she'd spoken into her and she wondered even now if she'd ever be able to forget it. She looked back at him when he said her name.

"I am so sorry that you were hurt by them. I paid them…well, they were supposed to give you everything your mother could not. And look what happened to you." He wiped at tears and she held his hand. "I failed so many people."

She tried to comfort him, but he was still so weak. When he told her about the house and that he'd been keeping it for her, she decided to go and see if any memories were there yet. She found it about an hour after leaving his cell.

The place wasn't run down nor was it in poor shape like she'd thought it would be. It was a two-story house that had a slate roof and a porch that went all the way around it. She walked up to the front door and used the key he'd given her. It slid in after a few tries and she went inside.

There was little furniture and what there was of it was covered with tarps. She removed them as she walked around the dusty room. Nothing with any padding would have survived, but the wooden couch and end tables sat in the room. There wasn't any electricity now, but there were two lamps as well as a television that sat in one corner. She moved on to the kitchen area after securing all the tarps again. This room was large, but not as big as the one she now had with Dallas. The refrigerator was empty and standing open, as were all the cabinets. The counters were dirty and he'd told her that, because of the scent of the wolf, he doubted that any rodents would enter the house and he appeared to be right.

Wolf's urine would keep away most smaller animals even if it was very weak.

There was another room, this one empty of anything more than two large corner cabinets that the glass was still in. She wondered if her mother had had pretty dishes in them or if she had simply used this room for affairs. The kitchen had a table and chairs that she would have used. She moved to the stairs and up them.

There was a bathroom here. The one downstairs held a laundry room that was also empty and had no shower. This one held a tub as well as a commode and sink. Peeking into the linen closet and finding it empty she moved to one of the bedrooms. It was a nursery.

The cradle was hand carved and she could almost see a child of hers in it. She ran her fingers over the smooth wood and wondered if Dallas would let her bring it to his...their home. She decided to ask him. The baby bed was handmade as well and though there were no blankets or mattress, she could see that it was made with love. The shelves on the walls were empty and she wondered what had been on them. She stepped closer to find that she had been mistaken. A small blanket was there still and it was wrapped around something hard. The blanket protected whatever was inside from the dirt. She opened it gently and pulled out the small book.

She was looking at the cover of the diary when she heard someone downstairs. She didn't go down yet, but waited to see if she could figure it out before she got herself killed. She smiled when she thought of what her mate would say if she even got hurt. He was very protective of her.

"As I should be. Where are you?"

His voice startled her and she moved back against the wall when he'd seemingly spoken right next to her.

"I didn't mean to frighten you, love, but I wanted to see you."

"I am at my mother's house. There is someone downstairs that I cannot smell. I think it is a vampire. Where is Phil?" She was not afraid, but she was beginning to feel uneasy.

"He is with me. I'm coming. Stay hidden until I get there. And for your sake, you'd better be in perfect shape when I get to you. It will make spanking you so much more pleasurable."

The stairs creaked and she waited near them out of sight. There were three rooms up here, but none that she wished to be trapped in. When she saw the person, a woman, she nearly attacked when she realized that she was unable to smell her. And waiting for her mate was no longer an option when she turned to look at her.

"Hello." She put out her hand, but Stacy did not take it. She was trapped but far from without means. "My name is Melissa Benjamin. I don't believe we've ever been formally introduced."

A small noise was all the warning she had before Phil and Dallas appeared in the hall with them. Stacy was not sure why, but she felt suddenly protective of the older woman and stepped in front of her between the two males.

"Wait, Dallas. Something isn't…" Phil looked from one to the other of them and smiled at Stacy. "I think you've just met a relative of yours. Am I right?"

"Yes," Melissa said with a smile. "I'm your aunt on your father's side. He's not…I don't remember the last time I saw him, but when I saw you come in here, well, I knew immediately who you were."

"You've been stalking her?" Dallas moved to her side and she wanted to smack him upside the head. "You should know that, as her mate, I will kill you if you think to take her to that fucktard."

"Fucktard? I don't believe I know…it doesn't sound as if that's a nice term. Am I to believe that Richard is up to his old tricks again and has managed to piss off some very prominent people?" Melissa shook her head. "He was forever doing that to people he tried to impress. Who are you and what do I need to pay you for you to kill him off?"

Stacy looked at her supposed aunt then at the other two men. She was confused, but more than that, she wanted to ask questions. Dallas put his hand around her and pulled her body to his. Comfort surrounded her and she felt calmed by the move. And just like that, she knew.

"He did not know about you. He thought himself to be an only child and you are a sister he does not know." Melissa nodded. "And you are as I am. Without scent."

"Yes. I met you once a long time ago. Your mother and I were very close and she'd have me over when Richard was away. I wasn't worried he'd find out, you see, because of what I am, but your mother worried so. When she died…when she died, I felt as if a large hole had been put into my heart." Melissa reached out and moved a strand of hair from her forehead and smiled sadly. "You look like her. I nearly didn't…I thought you a ghost when I saw you walk into this house."

"But you said you'd pay to have him killed." Phil looked at all of them as he spoke. "I'm willing to bet you know something that others might not."

"He killed his mate when she told him she was leaving him."

Stacy felt her heart constrict.

"I'm sorry, child, but she was doing it for you."

"Let's take this to our home." Dallas held onto her and glared at Phil. "I'll walk this time, thanks. It's nearly too much to ride with you."

Phil laughed as he headed down the stairs. "I have a great time every time I carry one of you wolves for the first time. You should have seen—" He stopped suddenly and looked back at them. "Stacy, when you told Dallas someone was here, you said vamp. Why?"

"I thought I smelled…blood. Why?"

He shook his head and told her that he would explain later.

"Phil, what's going on? What do you know about this place?"

He looked up at them from the bottom stair and then at her aunt. She knew something was going on, but not what. He continued to stare at her until they both looked up at her.

"Your aunt is part vampire, as you said. And if you can smell her, blood, as you said, then she's more than I thought." He looked at Melissa hard. "How much and why now?"

She didn't look as if she was going to answer. Melissa looked at the door for so long that Phil stepped in front of it. She looked up at her before looking back at Phil.

"He told me if I found her he'd let my family go. I don't…they aren't day walkers like me, but true night shadows. I can't let him kill them."

"So you were to bring her to him and then what?" All Melissa did was shrug at Dallas' question. "How much did he pay you?"

"Nothing," she nearly shrieked. "He has my family. I swear to you." Phil reached out to touch her and she shrank back. "Please don't. He'll know that you've touched me."

"No he won't because you're not going back to him." Phil's voice was hard and unforgiving. He put his hand to her head and seemed to stiffen from the touch. When he finished Melissa dropped to the floor without a sound.

"Come on. We have to get the hell out of here right fucking now." He grabbed both her and Dallas and suddenly they were moving. She felt her belly lurch and Dallas pulled her head to his chest.

~~~

Phil was pissed. He should have scented that something was off, but had nearly waited too long to see it. Thankfully Stacy had been smarter than him. He walked around the yard several times hoping to calm himself before he went back into the house. The vampire from the house was currently with his parents.

"If you don't stop that I'm going to have to hurt you."

He looked up at Austin, who was leaning against the column to his porch.

"You just have to realize that wolves are by far smarter than vampires and you won't be so disappointed when it hits you between the eyes."

"Fuck off. She could have been killed. Or worse, she could have been taken by that vampire and we'd never know it."

Austin shrugged.

"You mean you don't care that she was a paid assassin by your rival?"

"Oh I care all right. But this is the new me. The more 'in touch with my inner self' alpha." He grinned. "What do you think?"

"I think it's stupid. Where did you come up with that lame-brained idea? Reading one of those girly magazines for help?"

Austin growled low.

"Oh no, let me guess. Your mate. CJ decided that you needed to be self-aware and now you're a pussy instead of a wolf?"

"Yes, it was her idea and until you came along and fucked it all up, it was working for me." Austin stretched his neck. "Not really, but it makes CJ happy so I was willing to give it a try. Tell me what you know about the imposter."

"She's not. An imposter, I mean. She really is being blackmailed by Rich. And he really does have her family. Her human mate as well as their household. He gave her as much information as he thought she'd need except for one thing. Stacy's ability to smell a vampire."

"I don't understand. Can't anyone smell one of you guys? Especially if they're not human?"

Phil shook his head.

"I can smell you."

"Yes, because we're friends. But a normal wolf, one without contact with one of our kind, wouldn't know what we smell like. I bet if you asked any of those people you brought here if they could smell her they'd tell you no. Stacy, because of her inability to be scented, has a little extra nostril power."

Austin sat down on the steps and looked to be processing what he was telling him. That's why he liked the big man. He never went off half-cocked. Phil moved to the steps and sat beside him.

"You're saying that because of our friendship we can have a certain ability over a lot of other wolves? That not only can we smell you, but you can't hide from us as easily?"

Phil nodded.

"How was she able to hide her scent from me then?"

"She can mask her scent, as can I. But she didn't fool Stacy because of what she is. And what she is can be something very useful to you if you want to employ her to use it."

"No." Dallas came out of the house and glared down at the two of them. "You'll not use her in any way, shape, or form. I'll not have my mate used as bait so that we can catch the bastard that sired her."

"I don't think you have much say in that, buddy. You're going to have to do better than that if Stacy has any say in this." Phil nodded to the doorway. "And a great deal of explaining to do if her face is any indication."

Stacy stood there looking like fury, if fury had a face, that is. Phil could see the tension in her body and her eyes had turned. He'd been around Holly when she'd been nearly this pissed and didn't envy Dallas her anger at all. She simply walked between him and Austin and toward the tree line. Phil put his hand out to stop the man before he could follow.

"If I were you, I'd wait. I've seen pissed off mates before and she looks to have murder in her eye. And right now, I can't blame her."

Dallas jerked away from him, but not when Austin grabbed him. "You'll stay here. She's going to see Alexis and she said to wait."

Phil looked at Austin with a raised brow.

"Alexis just contacted me. She said Stacy is on her way there and that she didn't want anyone to come over just yet."

Dallas looked torn. He wanted to go to his mate and he also couldn't go against his alpha. Phil would have said fuck it and had the shit knocked out of him for his effort. Holly could be a mite mean when she needed to be. Phil smiled. But the makeup sex was phenomenal.

Dallas went to the yard and watched her disappear into the trees. He looked so hurt that Phil almost felt sorry for him. He looked at them as he spoke. "She's been so hurt by all this. I don't want anything to happen to her. I've fallen in love with her and I can't stand to see her hurt anymore." He looked at the trees again. "If that were your mates, you'd go after her, right?"

"Hell no," both him and Austin said nearly at the same time. "You have to give them their space or they make living with them unbearable."

Phil nodded at Austin's advice before adding his own. "She's used to doing things her own way and at her own pace. If you want her to be happy then you need to back the fuck up, as your sister is so fond of telling me."

Both men laughed at him. "I'm glad to see that Holly isn't letting you push her around."

Dallas laughed at Austin's observation. "And I'm glad you know not to push when she doesn't need you."

Phil laughed and agreed with her brothers. He almost added the part about the makeup sex, but decided that he might need Holly here to protect him if he did that. Then again, she might help them hurt him.

Phil smiled again. Oh yeah, this family was a great deal of fun.

Chapter 12

The notebook was not what she'd expected. There were dates and notes under them, but nothing…she handed it to Alexis. She'd wanted her mother's thoughts, not everything her father had done to her mother when they'd been married.

"She tells of the night you were born."

Stacy nodded.

"And she says that your father didn't show. He was on some kind of hunt, but your mother says he was with another bitch. Several it seems."

"He still does that. Goes to several women at the same time." Stacy looked at one of the cubs sleeping on the couch while the other played quietly near the table where the two of them sat. Stacy really liked Sis, but it was Jake that held her heart.

"He beat your mother a great deal, it seems. Nearly to her death a few times."

Again Stacy nodded but said nothing.

"Why would she leave you this, or would someone leave it behind for you to find?"

"I doubt my uncle knew it was there and my father had already changed his name by then so no one thought I would come back to the house. I guess it might have been overlooked." She ran her finger down the soap they were currently wrapping for Alexis' store. "But it is not that information I think she meant for me to have. It is the information in the back."

Stacy brought the soap to her nose and inhaled deeply. Lavender and oats, as well as some aloe were what this bar smelled of. She wrapped it up in the parchment paper with Alexis' logo all over it and reached for another bar. This one smelled of chamomile and honeysuckle. She continued to wrap the product as Alexis read.

"It says here that nearly all the land your mother owns is yours. And has been since your mother's death. I'm not sure, but I think that makes you an alpha person over your father."

She looked at Alexis when she didn't continue.

"Doesn't that mean that you can order him around?"

"Yes, by pack law. But when I mated with Dallas everything I am became his as well. He is now a pack leader over my father because Dallas is my mate." Stacy knew it was much more complicated than that, but did not really know all the rules.

"Does Dallas know this?"

Stacy shook her head.

"Are you planning to tell him? I think this might be important enough to get over your anger with him to let him know."

Stacy looked at her. "Are you commanding me to do this?"

Alexis looked away and Stacy knew that she was going to say yes. She was not sure if she wanted her to say yes or no, but she did not want to talk to her mate right now.

"I don't know what to do. You should tell him, but I hate it when Gordon gets all bossy with me too. I think it's in their DNA or something." She picked up the next bar of soap and started to wrap it. "But you should tell Austin. He's my alpha and if you don't I will have to tell him."

Stacy knew that too. She thought maybe that she'd been counting on Alexis telling her that as well. Stacy stood up and walked to the door. Alexis stopped her by saying her name.

"If I were you, and I know that I've not been with this pack long, I would tell Dallas. He'll find out eventually and finding out from someone else other than you might make him madder at you." Stacy turned toward the door. "And Stacy, the makeup sex is awesome."

Still grinning, she went out of the shop. Stacy did not want to go home yet, but she did want to speak to Dallas. She found a place to hide and laid low to be able to watch and talk to him.

"If you yell at me then I will not speak to you." She was pretty sure that he had not contacted her because he was waiting rather than her being able to block him out. She did not know much about this mate business.

"Okay. But you have to tell me that you're safe. I can't stand the thought of you being in harm's way." She could hear the anger in his voice, but not so much that it made her not want to speak to him.

"I am fine. I have found a book that I would like to discuss with you. It concerns the territory my father claims as his." She wanted to tell him she'd give it to him now, but waited to see if he would demand it. *"The land belonged to my mother's family and, as she has been killed, it belongs to me."*

He was quiet for so long she thought him to be not speaking to her. But when he did speak it was not with anger at all. *"So he is living off your good graces. What do you want to do about it?"*

She felt her pride in him swell. Stacy pulled out the little book and read a passage to him. *"My mother wrote that she believed him to be lying about his name. She said 'I think my mate is a liar as well as a thief. I heard him tell another of our pack that someday he'd be rich as any wolf even if he had to kill all he knew to get it. When the other man, a man called Jacobson, asked him why he needed to be so rich, Richard said why not? I believe he will do just as he said.'"*

"Jacobson, as in the man on the Council of Wolves Jacobson?"

She told him that it did not say.

"It seems that your father had it in good with a great many people. Could be why he felt he needed so much money. He could pay off who needed to be and have enough to run with if it became necessary."

Stacy believed him. Her father, from what she had heard from others, was a man who always had an angle and seemed to talk a big game. She wondered if he had ever thought of her over the years.

"If I am able to help I would like to be able to. It is important to me that my father is not a threat to any more people, especially those that cannot protect themselves."

He didn't answer her and she stayed where she was. It was one thing to be told what she could do. It was a matter altogether different to be told she could not help when it was necessary.

"They think that you can sneak into his lair, wherever that might be, and kill him. I think it would be hard to kill ones' own sire. But if you insist then I would ask that you let me go with you. I wouldn't be able to sit by while you go off somewhere you could be harmed."

She liked that he was asking, but couldn't see how it would work. *"I have no scent. However, you do. If we go together, then you will get us harmed."* Probably killed, but she did not say that.

"Come home, Stacy. I need to hold you." She felt his need like it was her own…it became her own. *"If you come home now, the house is empty and I'll make it well worth your while."*

She laughed. She couldn't help it. He was such a good man and she loved him very much.

"I will come home if you let me have my way with you first. You are always in such a hurry that I do not get to explore." She felt his growl. *"You are making me wet, Dallas."*

"Come here now, Stacy Force. I'll let you play all you want, but in the end I'm going to fuck you hard."

Stacy stood, suddenly wanting to get to him now. She turned toward their home and shifted. She could make better time as a wolf.

~~~

Rich didn't like the way the alpha spoke to him on the phone. He was taunting him, plain and simple. Rich went to the kitchen and looked at the casserole he'd put into the oven before he'd left. He didn't have a clue what it was supposed to be, but as he'd already eaten all the other things this and five other of the same brown and green stuff was all that was left.

He looked down at the overflowing trash can and decided that he'd better figure some things out while he was here. Where the trash went was one thing, as well as running the washing machine that was in a smallish closet off the kitchen. He wished he'd been smarter in taking this house and looked for one that had a male in it about his size. The tiny woman had had nothing he could wear and now he had to wash the only pair of pants he had.

He'd brought the mail in this morning and found that, while he knew her name, he didn't have a clue what she'd done for a living. Did he call her work? Was someone going to come to the house to figure out where she was? He didn't think she worked, there was no car in the tiny garage, and the mail she got was mostly contests she'd entered and lost and a few bills. Rich was going to send money in for her electric tomorrow. He didn't want to be caught without that again. The cave had been bad enough.

As the food cooked, which was now starting to smell like he'd picked a dessert rather than a meal, he pulled out the notebook he'd found when searching for money or anything to get him by. The stupid thing had numbers in it, not the phone kind, but like she was playing a game that required her to keep score. He didn't have any idea what "Uno" was and didn't really care. But if one were to get the lowest score, she would win hands down.

The paper was divided into three sections. He'd marked one "alpha," the next one "discretions," and the final one he'd marked "paid." So far, all he'd been able to put into the first column was "stole pack and money" and "burned me out." He'd put "fat" on there as well, but had marked through it. It wouldn't be fair with all the other things he was going to make Alpha Force pay for to add things he really had no part in. The meal started to smell odd and he went to the oven.

As always, it was times like these that he missed Harvey. He'd been doped up all the time, but he kept his brother fed. He'd done the man a favor, he'd been thinking, by killing off his mate. Harvey had become quite the cook and he'd been one hell of a house cleaner. He took the now crisp…thing to the table and started to eat.

"Mother fuck," he screamed when the roof of his mouth burned. "Another thing for you, Alpha Force." And he added this to his list as he nursed his burning mouth. "I'm going over the deep end here, don't you think?" He nodded at his question. "I'm talking to myself, but not yet answering me yet. So I guess that can rule out insanity."

Rich laughed and went to the cabinets to find them once again empty. He remembered going to the store, but not what he'd bought. Going to his list again, he wrote "Stealing my food." Then for good measure he added, "pain in my ass" to his list. Sitting down, he looked at the "paid" column.

The only things he had there were buried bodies on land and burned out relative. He was pretty sure that the two men were related, he just didn't know at the moment.

"But you can bet your last dollar I'll figure it out." He picked at the burned food again. "'Course you got all my dollars."

Rich watched the television without sound. He was hearing voices now and he wasn't always sure it was him. He'd caught himself twice now almost answering himself, but had nipped that in the bud right away.

"Yes I did, nipped it right in the bud." Laughing again, he nearly pissed himself when the phone rang. He wasn't sure if the old woman in the shoe had an answering machine—he laughed at the nickname he'd given her—so he listened carefully to hear for it. The voice spoke from the phone itself and for some reason, he thought it the funniest thing in the world.

"Mabel, you need to turn in that book you borrowed from the liberry. They're other people that wanna read it, you know. Don't you think a month is long enough to have it? Give it up, girl, that man on the cover isn't going to pick you no matter how many times you read it from cover to cover."

Rich went up to the bedroom where he'd been sleeping and looked around for the book to take back. He didn't want anyone coming here unexpected-like and he thought maybe the woman on the phone needed it a tad bit more than Mabel did at the moment.

"Yeah, she doesn't have any light in the freezer unless I open it up for her. 'Course I think maybe I broke her reading glasses when I snapped her neck, but what the fuck? She'll take the stupid book back to the *liberry* for you." Stupid hick town.

Rich was suddenly glad he'd had nothing to do with the humans here in this shit hole town and pulled open drawers to find the book when he nearly fell back on the bed. There in the nightstand was a gun.

And not just a little old lady one either. It was a Glock nine millimeter. He pulled it out and looked it over. Loaded with silver. The old bat might have known about his kind, it seemed.

"Gotta add that to another list. Killed off a human who knew about us. Can't have that, can we?"

"Nope. Can't." He looked around the room for the voice. *"You know it's me, you idiot. You said you were going over the edge. I'm here to help you."*

"So now I'm answering myself." He felt himself nod and felt the hair on the back of his neck rise. "Okay then prove you're not here talking to me."

"Prove what? That you're a nut ball? Get over it. Take that gun and put it in your pocket. Next time you come across that fucking bastard Force, blow a hole in his head." His other self seemed to have his shit together.

"You should come work for me. I need a cook and a housekeeper. I'll pay you really well. My brother took off and—"

"You know Force has him, right? He took him and is now brainwashing him. In a few more days, he'll think you killed all those people and you stole all their money." Rich nodded again. *"And now that you have your little equalizer, you can hunt the prick down and take his fucking ass out."*

He liked that idea more and more. Hunt the man down and kill him. He would be a hero. The man had killed a lot of people to steal his money and he wasn't going to let him take any more.

"You know where he is? All I've been able to find is where somebody with the last name is. Of course I know where his territory is, but I can't enter it without permission." He waited until his other self stopped laughing. Suddenly, he didn't like the other person.

"You don't need permission, you got Mr. Equal. And if you have no need for permission then you can simply go there and kill them all until you get the right one."

Rich laughed. "Thanks. Next time you need help, you let me know. You're all right."

Rich went to find his directory and realized it had burned up in the house too. After conferring with his other, he was trying to think up a good name for himself when one of them suggested the phone book. He was looking it over when someone knocked at the front door.

CHAPTER 13

Dallas opened the door when he heard her on the porch. She looked winded and wild, just the way he liked her. She smiled shyly at him.

"You ran here." He flushed when he realized how stupid that sounded. "I've been busy since we talked."

"Where did you send everyone? I didn't think the houses were done as yet."

He shook his head.

"Then you've thrown them out?"

He laughed. "No. Some of them decided to stay at Phil's." He didn't tell her that they'd found out they were newly mated and nearly knocked him over to get out of the house. "He had to promise them that he'd not feed from them, nor would he eat their children. The things people believe."

He'd been little better when he'd found out about the vampire. Phil was nice and all, but he'd been terrified of him at first. Then when he'd found out that Holly was his mate, he'd been a little on edge with him. But Phil had saved CJ's life as well as a few other friends of theirs.

She nodded and stood on the porch still. He moved to the side and hoped she'd enter on her own. For as much as he wanted to drag her to the floor and take her, he knew she needed him to give her something more tonight. And he'd tried.

Stacy moved into the living room of their home and stood back. He'd tried to clean up before everyone left, but again, as soon as the women staying there found out, they'd moved through the house like a tornado. He probably had the cleanest house in five counties. But the added touches made him hope she wasn't going to think he was a sap.

She walked toward the kitchen where the first of their night together was to begin. He darted ahead of her to take the steaks out of the oven when the timer went off. He pulled out her chair and asked her to sit.

"I had help with dinner. I'm not a great cook, but I can cook some things. Tonight's dinner was courtesy of the ladies. They gave me instructions on how to put our plates together." He held up the list and then turned to take the salad out of the fridge. "I have wine too if you'd like." He had to rub his hands on his jeans. Suddenly, he was completely out of his element and over his head. He took a deep breath and looked at his notes. *Stay calm and talk softly.*

So far, so good.

He tossed the salad with the dressing and glanced over at her. She was watching him intently. He wasn't sure if it was because she was waiting for him to mess up or if she was thinking he might poison her. He hoped not. He wanted her to be with him for the rest of their days.

He looked at the note again. *Small talk.* What the hell was that? Talking in short sentences? He knew that wasn't it, but he did smile at her and tried to think of one thing to say.

"Phil thought maybe he could find the alpha of the other pack now that he had his scent." He cringed when he said that. *Right, you big idiot. Remind her that she has no scent.*

"I had heard that he had looked for him. What is it I can do to help you? I feel like I should be doing something." He shook his head. "At least let me pour us some wine?"

He handed her the bottle that Phil had brought over. He said it was already breathing, but to leave it out and serve it at room temperature. Breathing wine? Small talk? He was going to fuck this up.

He managed to get the plates looking reasonably nice. He had slopped a little bit of the butter onto the steak, but it had melted so fast he didn't think she'd noticed. And the parsley he'd been told to put near the steak looked a little wilted, but he was fine with that too when Stacy smiled at him.

"It is very lovely." She took one of the rolls he'd had to cut the bottom off of when he'd gone to open the door for her and had forgotten about. "Hum, this is very nice, Dallas. I have not eaten all day."

"Thanks. I just hope you don't get too sick from this." He looked at her when she cut the steak and sighed with relief when she actually could. He'd been terrified it would have been as tough as his boots.

"I have been thinking about what your brother has said. I believe that he is correct in thinking that I could help with capturing my father." She was cutting her potato up so she missed his flash of anger, for which he was glad. "I would also like for you to go with me as far as we can so that you are close if something should go wrong."

That made him stop with the fork halfway to his mouth. "You want me to go? I thought you were mad at me because you didn't want me to be around because of…well, because."

"I did not say that. I said I thought it a good idea for you not to go. I think if you stayed back and away then I could go in and do whatever it is they think I can do. If there is a problem then I could easily call for you."

He liked that idea and finished his bite before answering her. For some reason he didn't want to get his hopes up that she may actually need him. He frowned when she laughed.

"What's so funny?" He grinned when she shook her head. "I'm making an effort here. Tell me."

"Okay. First, I love you. I have never said that to anyone before, but I do. Secondly…secondly, this is the worst meal I have ever eaten." She laughed again and showed him the bottom of her steak and the undercooked places in her potato. "Also I do not know who helped you make this, but they should be barred from the kitchen."

He looked down at his own meal. She was right. He picked up one of the rolls and tossed it at her. She ducked, but some of the blackened part of it sprinkled on her face. She picked up her potato and threw it at him, sour cream, butter, and all. After that, it was an all-out war.

When he ducked from the steak, he charged her. Taking her to the floor, she smashed one of his rolls in his face and then smeared butter all over his hair. He had to work to grab her hands, but when he got them together and above her head, he held her down with his body.

"You're going to pay for that, girl. I worked really hard on this dinner to romance you."

She licked his nose and grimaced at the taste.

"And I hope you know that you're cleaning this mess up."

"Really? I do not think so." She wrapped her legs around his and then her arms around his neck. "How about we toss for it?"

"Toss what?" He was having a hard time concentrating on what she was saying the way she kept shifting under him. If she kept that up he was never going to make it upstairs to their bedroom. "I have a surprise upstairs for you."

She pulled his mouth to hers. The kiss was soft and too brief, but held a lot of power. "I like it here. And I still want to explore you. You said that I could." She ran her fingers down his neck to his shoulders. When she tried to push him over he allowed himself to be turned and she straddled him. She sat over his waist and fingered the buttons on his shirt.

"May I unbutton this from you?" Her voice was heavy, yet low. He could feel her need now and his body was feeding from it. He nodded at her question.

"Yes. What is it you want from me, love? You want me to lay here and let you touch me, or do I get to touch you as well?" He wanted to touch her, but also knew that if he started he'd take over, and he desperately wanted her to touch him.

"I would like for you to guide me to pleasuring you. I want to touch, explore. I would like to taste your skin on different areas of your lovely body." She unbuttoned the first three buttons. "I would like to try riding you. I have heard that it is an experience that one does not forget."

Her words did not match the woman that sat over him. While what she said was seductive and bold, her hands and body showed a woman without knowledge of what she wanted.

"It won't be for us. I have to be naked for you to ride me, as do you." He reached up to pull her shirt over her head and tossed it behind him. "Scoot down to my thighs and I'll undo my pants."

"I will do it." She moved down to where he'd told her to and held his breath when she undid his belt and then the snap on his trousers. When the zipper went down and her fingers brushed across his hard cock, he hissed out in pain.

Lifting his ass from the floor, she took his pants to his calves, but left them there. Before he could tell her how to proceed, she was wrapping her cool hand around his cock. He actually felt his eyes roll to the back of his head.

"You are thick, are you not? And not at all what I had thought a man would look like. It's like velvet over steel, yet you are so sensitive here as well." He growled when she lowered her head to his cock and licked. "You taste of male. Nature as well. I love the feel of your tongue when you take me. It is so stimulating."

"If you stimulate me much more, I'm going to finish way before I wanted to." She leaned down and took his engorged head into her mouth. "Stacy."

She took his breath away. And if he died right here, right now, he'd be a very happy man. Before he could stop himself he wound his fingers into her hair and held her to him tighter.

When she let his cock go he could see her wolf crawl along her skin. His wolf responded as well. Letting go of her hair in case he pulled her back down, he fisted his hands at his sides.

"I would like to ride you now." She moved up his body, narrowly missing his balls before she settled over him once again. When she wrapped her fingers around him again and slowly lowered herself over him he didn't move. Didn't so much as breathe. Afraid that he'd come with even the slightest touch of her, he rocked up into her and stilled.

His shirt came open the rest of the way. Her body moved in jerky movements at first so he wrapped his hands around her tiny waist and showed her how to move so that they both enjoyed it.

She was an incredibly fast learner and soon he was hanging on so that when he came, he didn't shatter into a million pieces.

"I'm coming." Her shout of release caught him by surprise and when she stiffened over him, throwing back her head, he watched her orgasm take her. She was the most beautiful thing he'd ever seen. When she collapsed over him he lifted her head by her hair and looked at her dark eyes.

"I'm not nearly finished with you."

She grinned at him.

"I would love to take you upstairs and take you there, but I need to finish what you teased me to."

"I would love that very much." Before she could say anything more he rolled her to her back and settled between her legs. "My, but you are very fast."

"Nope. Not with this. I'm going to go as slow as I can, but I'm telling you right now, I want to pound you until you can't walk."

She hummed her approval. "That sounds very nice. What do I need to do for a good pounding?"

He stopped moving. Not because he wanted to, but suddenly there was no blood in any other part of his body but his cock. He could see her down on her knees and him behind her. He rolled off her so quickly that she whimpered.

"On your knees and lower your head to the floor." Urgency was evident in her speed. She was in the position he'd imagined and her ass was right in front of him. "I'm going to fuck you like this, then I'm going to come deep in your pussy."

"Oh yes. I would like that very much."

His cock was straining almost to reach her and he fisted it as he moved up behind her. Sliding into her heat he felt her tighten around him. It wasn't enough and he needed her now. Grabbing her hips, he pulled her flush to him. Christ, he wasn't going to last long.

Moving in and out of her, he watched her breasts swing to and fro. Wishing he could pull one of her hard nipples into his mouth and nip at her, he leaned down and laced her fingers into his as he took her nearly to the floor.

"Dallas, please. Help me, please, to come. I need to have a release." He moved his hand down her body and then into her soaking curls between her legs. One touch of her clit and she screamed out his name.

He felt her milking him and, try as he might, he couldn't have stopped from joining her if he'd had a gun to his head. When his release came he threw back his head and howled. Then lowered his head to her shoulder and bit.

~~~

Waking when he picked her up, Stacy snuggled into his arms. She loved this man and would do anything he wanted. And if he ever wanted to let her explore him again, she would take him up on it. His chuckle made her realize that she'd been talking out loud.

"You missed this." He still held her as he turned on the light. At first she didn't see what he'd done to the room, but after a few seconds, it all became clear. He'd actually been trying to seduce her.

There were roses on the bed, hundreds of petals, as well as about a dozen roses. And not just red ones either, dark purples and blue, yellows and white. There was a mixture of the blooms on the bed as well. And in the middle of the pillows there was a single red rose.

The fireplace fire was dying down. She could feel the warmth all over the room and that's when she found the bottle in the champagne bucket. As well as a basket of cheeses and crackers and fruit.

"The ladies worked on the kitchen stuff and I worked up here. Phil helped with the champagne too. He said women liked to be wooed and that if I did this correctly he'd buy me a case. What do you think this goes for?" He poured her a glass and then showed her a bottle. "Since we both know how Phil is I'm assuming that he paid more than six bucks at the gas station for it."

Stacy laughed. He was trying to make up to her. But she'd long since forgiven him and had been meaning to tell him she'd been wrong. Maybe tomorrow. Or the next day. Alexis told her before she left the studio that keeping a man guessing was half the fun. The rest was a battle.

"Phil is very frugal, but he is not cheap. I like him. He is good to your sister." She crawled up the bed and yawned. "You have worn me out. I would love to have more of this wine, but I fear that I will fall asleep in the bubbles."

He took the glass from her and set both hers and his on the night stand. He stood her up and pulled back the sheets. "Here, you lie down and I'll be right there beside you. And in the morning, if you manage to be here when I wake, I will make it worth your while."

He wiggled his brows at her and she burst out laughing. "I will do that on one condition. You must not go down after I fall asleep and clean up our mess. We will need to get to it in the morning before any of your guests come in and see it."

He nodded as he stretched out beside her. "I love you, Stacy. More than I thought possible."

"I love you too, Dallas. And will for the rest of our days." She closed her eyes when she heard him snore. As soon as he had been asleep for a few minutes she turned her body to his and wrapped herself around him. He pulled her closer even in his sleep.

CHAPTER 14

Rich moved his gun to the back of his now clean pants. He was nearly to the Force place when he felt a familiar touch to his mind. He wasn't so much surprised as he was pissed off.

"I thought you dead." Hoped it, actually. It would save him the trouble of killing him himself. *"Where are you and how soon can you get to me? And by asking that, you know that I'm ordering you to come to me now."*

Rich didn't know where Harvey had been staying, but had an idea it had been with the Force's. He and Poor, the new name he'd given to his other self, had had a long conversation about Harvey, Austin, and the pack. Neither of them were very happy right now.

"I'm not coming to you. Nor will I ever. You have treated me badly for long enough. Now I do what I want."

Rich stopped in mid-step. He couldn't believe what his brother was saying.

"And so you know, the pack here is well aware of you living off the means of your daughter."

"I don't know what you're talking about. I had you kill her long ago. Things like her shouldn't be left to live." Rich moved to sit near a tree. *"You come to me right now and I won't make you suffer for it. As for my daughter, when this is*

finished, and it will finish soon, you'll do as I told you and murder the bad seed and bury her with that bitch of a mother of hers."

"Stacy has taken a mate. Would you like to know who the fates have chosen?" Rich tried to think who Stacy was and nearly asked him when he spoke again. *"Your daughter has done well for herself. And with the added property that has come to her she will bring a lovely dowry to her pack."*

"My daughter? I think not. Her mother laid with another. That abomination will never take my name." He had a moment of panic when he thought of his daughter, but dismissed it soon enough. *"Tell me who her mate is so that you can have your say and come here. I'm nearly to the—"*

"She is mated to Dallas Force."

Rich waited for the laughter. Waited in vain for the "just kidding," even though his brother had never had much of a sense of humor. But nothing was forthcoming.

"You lie." Rich realized he'd spoken out loud then spoke to his brother. *"You lie. Why would she mate with my mortal enemy? She would never do that to her own father."*

Laughter touched his mind. Something his brother hadn't done in, well, decades. Rich waited for him to calm before he spoke again. It was then that he realized that Harvey sounded almost sane.

"You tell me that she is dead to you in one breath then say that she wouldn't dishonor you, her father, in the next. You are going to have to do better than that, brother dear. And I do not lie." There was a hardness there, something that Rich had never heard from his younger brother. *"And the vampire you sent to kill her is now in the custody of the council. And they have retrieved her household."*

He'd forgotten about her. He couldn't recall her name at the moment, but he'd kidnapped her and had tried to kill her mate. The human had been much harder to get to than he would have first though. Humans, he thought, shouldn't be allowed to turn on wolves. They should be simply grateful that his kind let the human race live at all.

"She served her purpose." Rich stood up again and started walking toward the Force compound. *"I had a good fuck and now they know that I mean business."*

He'd not had sex with anyone really. He'd thought about it, but once he'd locked them all in the shed out back, he'd been so worn out that he'd barely been able to hold his head up. He'd ended up taking a nap on the cold ground and had waked only when he heard a car in the drive. He'd hidden while some pimply-faced kid had gotten out of the car and had knocked on the door. Rich supposed he'd been there to collect the paper bill. Stupid humans. They could actually watch it on the television. Why read it when it was unnecessary?

Harvey didn't answer him. Rich was afraid that his brother was really not coming to him. He needed him, more than he'd ever thought possible. He was about to beg him to come to the forest with him when Harvey spoke again.

"You'd do well to turn yourself in, Richard. You're only hurting yourself by doing what you're doing to everyone. The council may go easier on you if you only admit what you've done."

Over his dead body.

"It may come to that."

The connection closed almost as if a door had physically come down between them. Rich looked around to see if he'd spoken out loud and his brother had been close enough to hear him. But there was nothing, not even a squirrel or bird.

Something was wrong here. His brother seemed to have grown a backbone and was speaking to him as if he was better than them. Yes, Rich thought, something was definitely wrong here.

"Of course there is. Did you think that Force was going to sit around and wait for us to come and shoot him? I think not."

He wanted to glare at Poor, but didn't know how that worked. "Are you being smart with me? You know what I do to people who are smart to me."

"Yes, and look where that has gotten you. In the middle of nowhere, fat, lazy, and walking much too slow for us to ever get to where we're going before it snows. Move the fuck up a bit, will you?"

Rich started to walk again. He was suddenly not liking his other self and he told himself so. "You should have better respect for me. When I get this other pack I'm going to be rich again and where will that leave you?"

The laughter again made him pissed. He continued walking without saying another word to his other self until he got to the gates of the compound. The hum of electricity was enough to make his wolf snarl and back away.

"Now what? I can't crawl under it because I don't have the proper tools. I can't even go over it without killing myself." Then there is the added bonus of not knowing what's on the other side. He looked up and down the high fence and wondered just who this guy didn't trust.

"You? Or maybe...no, he doesn't trust you." Rich walked on. *"You do know that we could have shifted and been there in half the time, don't you?"*

"And been naked when we got there. Thank you, but I have no desire to be fighting and killing whatever person is on the other side of this fence while I'm buck naked." Rich thought he'd gotten the last word when he spoke again.

"And I suppose bringing extra clothes would have been out of the question. You did know that you were coming here, right?" Rich tried to clamp his mind down to his other self and couldn't manage it. *"Of course you can't, you moronic dick. I am you."*

~~~

Georgia was sitting in the kitchen when Dallas came down. He looked around and saw that, with the exception of the cup in front of her, everything was cleaned up and everyone was gone. He opened the refrigerator and took out the milk. She stood up and took it from him before he could pour himself a glass. She ordered him to sit.

"Your mate Stacy has gone to her alpha. She said that she has pledged to the woman who makes soaps."

Dallas nodded, took the glass, and watched as she took out eggs and bacon.

"I must speak my mind. If you don't mind."

He started to point out that she'd been doing that, but only nodded again. He wondered where his mom was and the rest of the people who'd been staying with them. The smell of bacon frying made him realize that he'd not eaten much the night before and had burned a lot of calories. He flushed when he realized she was staring at him.

"You said you had something to say. Why don't you have a seat and tell me what it might be. I can't fix what I don't know is broken." He tried to smile at her, but she looked a great deal like his mother did when she knew he was shining her on. "I do want to help you."

"Rich isn't going to stop until you kill him." Okay, blunt worked too. "And when you do the council is going to come down on your heads for it, aren't they?"

"No. I don't know what they are going to do at this point. A rogue werewolf isn't something they want others to find out about. He is being hunted now as if he is going to be killed. No one will try to take him alive after what they've seen he's done to his pack."

Georgia nodded as she set his plate in front of him. "I want to know what your brother has planned for us. There are a few that want to leave now before Rich kills your brother and others still that want to help this pack so that they have a better chance of staying."

"Everyone can stay. Austin is a good man and he'd never turn anyone away. But if some of you want to leave then...I suppose we can make some arrangements for them to go to other packs." Dallas started eating and was surprised to find not only eggs, bacon and hash browns, but fluffy biscuits as well as gravy to smother it in. He moaned when he ate a few more bites. "You should open a restaurant. This is fantastic."

She got up and started cleaning the spotless sink. She tossed the rag in it and turned to him. "Can I? I used to do it. Run my restaurant. But when it started to lose money because Rich was taking all the profit and then some, it began to fail. Soon I couldn't even pay the employees or the bills and we had to fold."

It took his mind a few seconds to catch up. Unfortunately, by the time it did, Georgia had taken his silence for a no. She started talking about what a bad idea it was and that she'd never be able to make it work anyway.

"You can do whatever you want, Georgia. In fact, there is a building in town that I think you'd be able to make work for you." He tried to think what a restaurant would need and decided to ask someone in the college to help them. "After this is over why don't we sit down with Austin? You come up with a plan. You know, a menu and how much startup capital you think you'll need. The pack will help you start it, but you'll be ultimately responsible for it."

She was nodding and smiling. He thought she was going to hug him several times, but checked herself whenever she got close. He thought she was the happiest he'd ever seen her.

He grinned. "In the meantime, do you think you could fix us some meals here? Stacy doesn't cook and if you cleaned up from last night you know that I can't either." Something else occurred to him. "Maybe you could bring in a couple of people to work for us after you get the restaurant going. That way you can train someone to help you when you need them and I won't have to eat my own cooking."

This time she did hug him. It was quick, but he felt it all the way to his heart. He looked up at the door when his mate walked in. She didn't say a word, but Georgia stepped back and flinched. Stacy only hugged her as well and sat down.

"Do you think it is possible that I get some of what he is eating?"

Georgia stood there for only a few seconds before she moved to the stove again.

"And I would like some sausage, please. I do not care for bacon."

"Yes, miss, of course. I will do—"

"Georgia? You have hugged my mate and gotten away with it today. The least you could do is call me by my name, please."

Georgia nodded and turned back to the stove again. But not before Dallas saw the tears in her eyes. He looked at his mate. *"You are a good woman. You could have harmed her for what she did."* Stacy took the last piece of biscuit from his plate. *"Hey, you'll get yours."*

She bit off a large piece. *"So will you. Do not let another woman hug you, Dallas. I am a very jealous woman and would hate to cause you harm because you have a big heart."*

"You'd like for me to be mean?" He smiled at her when her own plate was set before her. *"Perhaps you'd like it if I only touched you. Like I did last night."*

"That would be advisable for you." She flushed a deep crimson. *"Of course we could go our separate ways and you could have any woman you want taking you into her arms."*

He pulled her to him and kissed her. Devoured her mouth before he let her go. *"You're the only woman I want to touch, love. And all I will ever have. I love you."*

"And I, you." She finished her breakfast in record time as he drank his milk. *"We must go to speak with your brother soon. My uncle has played his part well. Richard has threatened him."*

As soon as they both stood to leave Georgia stepped up to Stacy. The two of them looked deeply into one another eyes before Georgia nodded. "You are the one they said he murdered, his daughter." Stacy nodded. "The other man, his brother? Is he yet dead? The drugs in his system were supplied by the other alpha."

"My father?" Georgia shook her head. "Then who?"

"He is your sire, child, not your father. He supplied him with the drugs." Georgia looked at him them at Stacy again. "I knew your mother. She was a good woman and did not deserve to die like she did."

"No, she did not. And my uncle lives. He is better now thanks to some of my mate's family. He asks of your children. He said that he was training them at one time, giving them help with the lessons of our kind before his mate was murdered."

"I will send them to him. They would enjoy seeing him. Thank you." Georgia wrapped her arms around Stacy. "You are like her in many ways. Your mother was a good person, as are you."

Dallas and Stacy walked out of the house. Neither said anything as they got into the car and they were nearly to the pack house when she started to speak.

"My fath…Richard needs to be gotten rid of and I would very much like it to be me. He has caused more harm than should be caused by one man. And he will continue to do so until someone murders him." She looked over at him when he turned off the engine. "I have spoken with your sister and she said that she would work with me on defense. She said that I have a good body and will not go down easily."

Dallas wanted to forbid her to do this, but even if she didn't fight her sire, she would be prepared for anything else. He pulled her into his arms and held her to him.

"The man will not go down without a fight. The simple reason he's gotten away with so much so far is because everyone was afraid to go against him. That isn't the case any longer." He pulled her back and lifted her chin so that he could see her. "But if you get hurt or dead I will never forgive you. I love you and would very much like to spend some time with you that doesn't involve fifty people in our home."

She nodded. "I would very much like that as well. We will need to make a plan for that." She looked to the house where there were already several people milling about the yard. "They will want more from Austin that he will not be able to provide. Some of these people have been harmed beyond simple neglect."

"We have some doctors coming in soon. And not just for the physical ailments. Austin is aware that some will need therapy, as well as someone they can talk to and meds. He will keep them healthy as well as happy."

"I have heard of the educational classes he has had set up. Some believe that he will bore easily with this and be like the man they have left. But I have told them that he is a fierce man and a good alpha. He will not let go until everything is settled." She looked back at him. "They are in love with CJ and Alexis. They are in awe of Holly."

Everyone loved CJ. And Alexis. Both were kind and gentle when necessary, but bears when one of them thought someone was being harmed. Holly would kick ass with very little provocation. He loved that about her too.

"You and I need to get this settled so that we can start our life together. I want to see you swollen with our child."

She looked up at him, panicky.

"You aren't going to worry about whether or not they have scent. You just worry about how much we're going to spoil them. All right?"

She nodded and looked away. "I am not worried that you will not love them. I do not want them to be ridiculed. I would leave with them if that were to happen."

"You won't leave me and, trust me, they will be cherished for who they are, not what they can do." Dallas looked over at her uncle as he walked toward them.

Harvey was looking better every day. Today he was wearing a short coat in deference to the cooler weather and Dallas could see that he was even starting to put on some weight. He waved and smiled at them as he came toward them.

"My brother just contacted me. He would very much like for me to come to him. He said that…" Harvey cleared his throat as he looked around. "He thinks that I owe him and is very vocal about it."

CHAPTER 15

Phil walked to the door then turned to go back to his desk. It wasn't until Holly giggled that he remembered she was in the room with him. He tried to glare at her, but she was simply too beautiful lying there with a light blanket over her still nude form.

"You should know that I get less and less work done when you're home. If you would have an office in the city I could get things done here and still have time to work." She stretched out and her breast slid free of the blanket. "Of course there wouldn't be as much fun in my day, just more work."

His cock leaped to attention and he was tempted to go back to the couch and show her just what she had done to him, but he did have a meeting. A meeting that he wasn't looking forward to.

"You do know that this council meeting is in ten minutes, don't you? I have to go and persuade some of these people to let us kill off a rogue that has been terrorizing the area for many years." She sat up and let the blanket spill to her lap. "Will you behave? You've already distracted me twice today."

Four times if he counted before they got out of the bed. Christ, but this woman was delicious. He wanted her again, but only stood still while she dressed. He laughed when she held up a pair of ruined panties.

"I will need to go and buy more of these. Do you have any idea how much these suckers cost?"

He grinned more.

"It's not funny, Phil. These things are twenty bucks a pair and you've ruined three pair of them today."

"I'll be more than glad to purchase you several hundred pair daily if you let me rip them from your body again." He watched her bend over to pick up her jeans and moaned. "Or better yet, simply don't wear them. I wouldn't mind that."

"No. Now tell me about this meeting. Why can't you just kill him and simply say you're sorry? You know, 'it's better to ask for forgiveness than to ask for permission.' Or so I've heard." He was pretty sure she used that one a great deal, but shook his head at her. "Why not? People do it all the time. I might have used it on occasion myself."

He didn't comment on her usage, but picked up the file he'd been looking for. He loved this house. He hadn't, not for a long time, but since Holly had moved in he'd been happier about a great many things. The fireplace, desk, and the books lined up were the treasures of this room, and then there were the pictures of the two of them together.

They'd taken a long honeymoon. And the pictures there on the shelf were the only ones that they could publicly show. Holly growled low when she turned to him. Damn it, she was fully dressed.

"Behave or you'll not be going anywhere." He started to remove his tie. "No. Damn it. I have to go to work too. Go now before we're both in trouble."

Sighing, he moved back to the door. "I should be home soon. The council is meeting in the castle and then there's this do afterwards." Phil nodded toward the outside. "I can see some of the pack out there. Would you mind asking them to stop marking my yard? I can smell it all through the house."

She was still laughing when he shut the door behind him. He really couldn't smell it in the house; werewolf urine was very lightly scented. But he loved to see her laugh. He had no doubt that when he did get home she'd have had them pee on everything, including the front door. Smiling, he walked outside. Life was good.

The meeting wasn't going as well as he'd hoped. Austin was yelling at them to simply get off their asses and do something. There were others, ones that were only secondary to Austin and himself, that had a great deal to say, but very little of it had anything to do with what the fuck was going on. Finally he stood up and several of those members took a step back. Smiling, and yes, he supposed showing a bit more fang than necessary, he walked to around the table.

"You want to preserve weres. Okay, I can understand that." Phil turned to the wall beside them and raised a hand toward it. "Well, good people, here is what the latest victim saw when this one moved into her home and tried to murder her and her small children. Thanks to one of my more…let's just call it advanced abilities, I can show you just what she saw through her viewpoint. Have a look at what she saw."

The blank wall exploded in violence. First, the door from Georgia's point of view exploded inward and five large black wolves bounded into the room. A small child, no more than a few months old, was lying on the couch sleeping and Georgia looked as if she was going to move toward him only to be stopped. When she looked down, two of the wolves were tearing into her leg. Rich Sterling walked into the room and strolled over to the couch.

"What do we have here? A babe, is it?" He picked up the child and held it gently in his arms. "I hate children."

The child sailed across the room and hit the wall. His screams were abruptly cut off when one of the other wolves grabbed him up in their jaws and bit through his tender belly. Georgia screamed and screamed until Rich walked to her and slapped her. For several seconds, there was nothing, then her eyes blinked open.

It was carnage. A little girl was being stripped down and fondled. Another child, no more than six, was being treated the same way. Then suddenly a large dark gray wolf entered the broken door and tore into the wolves nearest the children. One was killed immediately, the second one tossed across the room as if he wasn't nearly four hundred pounds of muscle and bone.

"Enough."

Phil didn't stop the rolling memory, but put out his other hand and the man who stood was gagged. Phil would make them watch if it was the last thing he did. The man struggled, but nothing more.

As the she-wolf that entered last moved around the room Georgia was moving toward her youngest child. She watched the female, but it was obvious that the child was more important. Then when she cradled him in her arms, she looked up at the alpha and the female.

"You know who I am? It's within my rights to murder this family for what their sire did to my pants." He lifted his pant leg up and there was a small amount of mud on the cuff. "Just who is going to clean this up?"

The she-wolf snarled and lunged. She didn't get a bite out of the wolf, but Georgia began to move toward her other children. She was nearly to them when she looked back at the two fighting.

The she-wolf attacked the wolf to the alpha's left and ripped his throat out. Blood sprayed over the man standing next to him and his white shirt was stained with it. She shook her head and more blood and gore made their way to his face, body, and clothing. The alpha started to move toward the she-wolf and she snarled at him, her hackles high and her claws tearing into the dirt floor.

"You'll pay for this. All of you will pay for this with your lives." He looked at the she-wolf before he moved toward the door. "I'm your alpha and I deserve to be treated as a king no matter what those fucktards on the council have to say about it. I rule here. I'm master to you all and you'll bow before me or die."

As he moved out the door Georgia looked around the room. Blood and carnage were everywhere. Her children, the girls, were wrapping in blankets. The she-wolf, who was actually Stacy, shifted and Phil stopped the memory.

"The babe was near death when he was brought to the home of the enforcer of the Force pack. His lungs were damaged as well as massive brain damage. Had I not been there he would have died within the hour. The daughters, the two that the alpha had already said were going to be mates to the two wolves that were there, were—"

"They were children. Not old enough to be mated to a male of their size."

Phil looked at the man and waited. It seemed to occur to him slowly.

"He ordered it? He actually ordered those men to take those children as mates?"

"Yes. And these two aren't the only ones. There are nearly fifty children like these that had been given...sold to the highest bidder to have as their mates." Phil snarled and his fangs dropped lower in his anger. "Would you like to see what they looked like when those same men finished with them?"

No one moved other than to shake their heads. Several of them put their hands over their eyes. Phil moved to the table again and sat down. He looked over at Austin who was wiping at his face. Phil knew the man was thinking of his own child as well as the little ones now staying at his and CJ's home.

"You've given us…you've given us plenty to think about, Sir Campbell," Councilman Briggs said in a shaky voice. He stood then sat down again. "We are giving you full rights to have him taken—"

"You can't make that decision on your own."

Phil looked at the man standing next to Briggs.

"You have to put it before a vote. Then there need be a committee and rules governing them. If you send them out then they'll murder him in his sleep. Rich is my friend and—"

The room exploded in magic. The walls seemed to expand and then settle again, but the woman in the room took all their attention away. She was magnificent in all her glory and everyone bowed before her. All except Phil.

"Mother, you do know how to make an entrance." She kissed his cheek then patted his head. "What brings you to this meeting that you couldn't make it to when I asked?"

"He did." She turned to the man who had tried to defend Sterling. "We sort of figured someone was feeding him information as well as giving him the top skim of the monies owed to this realm."

"Stealing too, Dwayne?" Phil tisked and reached for Austin's shoulder to signal him to stand. "Shame on you. What should we do with him, Sir Force? I'm thinking I'm very hungry."

The man stood up and backed away. He was pale and his eyes darted around the room quickly. Every being in the room could smell his fear. He was stopped by Phil's dad before he could get to the door.

"Why don't you have a seat, asshole? I think you might not be leaving anytime soon." His dad sat Dwayne in the chair and held him there. "You've interrupted a very lovely afternoon with my lady wife because of your stupidly. Now, tell these nice people what you've been up to and we'll kill you and be about our business."

~~~

Dallas watched the woman walking toward him. He wanted her right now, but there were simply too many people around for him to take her. Stacy seemed to sense what he was thinking and stopped moving a good hundred feet from him. He reached for her through their link.

"You should see what I'm seeing. Your breasts are moving in a way that makes my cock ache with need. The thought of taking your nipples into my mouth has me salivating. I want to strip you naked and lick every part of you, take your juices into my body and feast on you."

"Dallas, you know that there are many people about. What will they think of you if you cannot keep your hands from my body?" She grinned at him and ran her hands over her full breasts. *"They will think you a beast."*

His own beast stirred under his skin and three people turned to look at him. Dallas was beyond caring. He didn't move toward her, not because he didn't want to, but because he wasn't sure he could move. There was no blood in any part of his body but his groin.

"Come here, bitch, and let me show you what you've unleashed." She shook her head at him and his wolf snarled. *"Come here, Stacy. If I must chase you then you'll be very sorry."* He found he wanted her to turn and run. Dallas wanted her to strip, shift, and have him chase her. Christ, his

wolf was nearly taking him and, when he growled low, several people moved away. He wasn't going to be able to control him much longer.

She turned around and looked at him over her shoulder. Her smile said a great deal. *Come to me. Fuck me. Own me.* He was willing to do all three. When he stood up she moved away from him. When she was at the clearing, still a good fifty feet from him, he watched her strip down. Her naked ass was the last thing he saw before she shifted and took off. Dallas could do no more than follow.

The second his wolf saw her he moved with speed to get her. Her scent of arousal was strong, but his wolf didn't need it. He could see that she was ready the moment they came upon the small pond. She was bent over the log in front of her and her ass ripe for him.

His wolf came up behind her and licked her. Her juices were thick and he knew the moment he entered her they were both going to come. Dallas covered her and entered her deep. His claws dug in the ground as he fucked her hard. Leaning over her shoulder, he bit and bit hard. Her cry of pain made his wolf happy and he threw back his head and howled.

He rolled off her and laid down. It took him several minutes before he could move any more than that and he closed his eyes. Stacy moved near him and curled her body over his. Still panting, he licked her jaw. It wasn't long before they were both sound asleep.

When Dallas woke, Stacy was still near him, but they both had shifted back to human. He pulled her body over his and held her to him. He concentrated on the forest surrounding them and tried to think of what they had to do. Tonight, as a matter of fact.

"Will do you no good to dwell on what cannot be changed. We will get through this and then he will be gone from our lives." She lifted her head up and watched him from her perch on his chest, her chin resting on her hand. "He will die and things will be normal again. As normal as we can make it."

"But to have you do this…you've no idea what this does to me. To know that he could harm you." He could actually kill her, but he refused to think about that. "I don't want you to do this, but I know that it is our only way."

She was to contact her sire. Stacy knew that he had wanted her killed when her mother had been and they hoped that he hadn't changed his mind. Harvey had set it up so that his brother knew she was alive and that she was with a Force. He'd made no bones about the fact that he hated them all more than anything.

"I will be safe. He cannot smell me and, with you nearby, there is no way that he can harm me. Phil has told me that he will be close at hand as well. I cannot lose you any more than you can me." He held her tighter to him and she smiled. "You would like for me to be barefoot and whelping all the time, I believe."

"Hell yes. As soon as you hit your cycle then we will never leave our bed." He ran his hands down her back to cup her ass. "We should try and practice a bit before that time comes, don't you think?"

She sat up over him and settled her legs on either side of his hips. His cock was straining from his body. Stacy wrapped her hands around him and milked him. "You are so hard. And at the same time, very smooth." Dallas didn't move as she moved up and down his shaft. "I love the way you feel when you take me. You are thick enough within me that you fill me completely."

"Stacy, baby, please. I need to fill you now." She shook her head and continued what she was doing. "Then take me into your mouth. I want to fuck your pretty mouth."

"No. I think I would like to watch you come this way. I want to see how hard you spray within me." She leaned down and licked the pre-cum that was dripping from the tiny eye. "When you come, Dallas, I will rub your juices on me and know that you've marked me whenever I touch myself. Would you like that?"

"Christ, yes."

She moved so that she was over his thigh now and her knee very close to his balls. She started to ride him as she pumped him and he leaned up on his elbows to watch her.

Mesmerized, he watched her face and her hand. She was enjoying herself so much so that he tried to hold back. His cock was burning with the need to come and he reached out his hand to slow her. She moved his hand away and brought it to her pussy.

"Help me, Dallas. Help me to come." He slid his finger into her heat and she tightened her hand over his cock. When she started to ride him harder Dallas knew he was going to come with her. Pinching her clit, she tightened around him again and he came.

Heavy cream shot from him. As it covered her breast, chin, and belly, he continued to come. Every downward stroke had her gathering his come and making the slide quick. Putting his hand over hers he helped her milk him even as her pussy clenched around his fingers. He needed more and rolled her to her back and spread her legs.

"Christ, you're beautiful. I need to taste you." Leaning down, he sucked her clit into his mouth and put his finger into her sheath. Her fingers in his hair held him tightly to her.

When she came again, then again, he sat up. His cock was hard again.

He moved over her, her legs still wide, and slowly entered her just to his tip. She bucked up, but he held her down by her knees. He wanted this his way now. Watching her pussy take him and soak him, he moved in and out of her slowly. Dallas moved his hand down to just where her shoulders where and took her nipple into his mouth.

"Dallas, please do not tease me. I need this very badly." He looked up at her and could see that she did. "Please, give me all of you."

Dallas took her mouth as he buried himself to his balls. As her legs wrapped around his hips, he moved them until she moaned, then he reached down and cupped her ass. He slid his finger into her ass and moved in and out of her as he fucked her, devoured her. When she came this time, he moved his head for her. He wanted her bite; he wanted her to mark him as her own. As soon as her canines broke his skin he jettisoned into her and roared with his release.

Dallas was a marked wolf.

CHAPTER 16

Rich moved along the people in the mall and knew that they were staring at him. He wanted to simply go in, get some clothes, and then leave. He'd found the old woman's stash of money just this morning and was going to get something to wear other than the smelly pants he'd tried to wash yesterday.

He started the machine and was reading the bottle of detergent when he realized that there wasn't enough water in the machine. He tried to figure out the controls, but ended up breaking one of the knobs off when it wouldn't turn. Rich realized that he was to push it only after tossing the stupid thing across the room.

Then he'd put in too much of the powder. Way too much, as it turned out. There were soap bubbles pouring out of the thing when he'd turned from the upper levels and even now the kitchen floor was slippery and slimy in places. And he couldn't get the soap out of his pants no matter how many times he'd taken them to the yard to spray off. He had had to hang them over the line in the backyard and let them drip dry while he wandered around the house in a woman's shirt and towel.

"I tried to tell you." He ignored Poor. He hadn't spoken to him since yesterday when he'd laughed at his attempts to get into the Force compound. He shivered when he thought

about how close he'd come to being caught with his pants down and his ass showing. Who knew that the stupid thing was electrified and would shoot him across the forest like a rocket?

"You never listen to me even though you invented me. Why is that, do you think? Are you not speaking because you know that I'm so much smarter than you?"

"You are not." He looked around the store he'd gone into when everyone stared at him. He kept forgetting to speak to this other self via mind thing. He grinned when one woman grabbed her kid and took off out the door. "I'm not going to be good for business."

"I told you that the fence smelled funny. You don't listen to me. How is it that you expect me to help you when you don't listen?" Rich moved to the rack of men's pants. *"You keep getting any fatter and we'll need to shop in the tent department."*

"I'm under a lot of stress. How am I supposed to take my pack back without clothes?" Rich wasn't even sure he'd be able to do it with a suit and tie on. *"That man, Force, has a great deal to answer for."*

"Yes, he does, and one of them is fucking your only child." Rich tried to shy away from that. The thought of his child being old enough to have sex, much less having it with a Force, made his skin crawl. *"You know that that alone is enough to get him killed. And where is that man at on the council? Wasn't he supposed to call you back with what happened at that meeting the other day?"*

Dwayne Hopewell was a man he didn't care for. But like most that Rich kept around him, he served a purpose. His purpose was to provide him with cash and information. The council wouldn't be able to sneak onto his land without him knowing about it for weeks. And the cash? Well, that was because Mr. Hopewell had a nasty little habit of liking his sex a little rough. Actually, very rough.

"I don't know why he's not called back. I made sure he had my new number three times before I provided him with his merchandise." That was another thing. Where was his money? *"I should hear back from him soon. He still owes me for that bit of fluff I gave him for his pleasure."*

Rich shivered as he looked over the different pants. Pleasure was only one-sided usually when it came to sadist Dwayne. And he'd only gotten rougher as the years had gone by. Too many times he'd had to send Harvey in to pick up what was left of the person he'd sent to the were. And usually, it would take Harvey burning down the shacks Dwayne had them in to get rid of the evidence.

Rich flared his nose. There was a scent there, one he'd smelled before. He moved to the front of the store only to be stopped by a man in a uniform. He nodded toward the clothes in Rich's hands before he spoke.

"You gonna pay for them before you leave here?" The man crossed his massive arms over his chest and moved every time Rich did. "You stunk them up so bad now that you're gonna buy them. So be a good boy and go on over to the counter and pay up."

Rich let a little of his beast go to try and scare the man, but the guard only smiled and let his go as well. Rich whimpered. He hated cats and this weretiger was fucking huge. His canines were nearly as big as Rich's thumb.

"Like I said, you go on over to the counter and pay for those things before I gotta wipe the floor up with your nasty self." Rich thought about tossing them in his face for all of a second then the tiger raised his brow. "Go ahead. I've not had dog stew for months. Mighty tough, but I'll still kill you."

Rich moved to the counter and the guard followed. Rich paid nearly half of his cash for three pair of pants and a shirt he wasn't sure was going to fit him. After the cashier handed him his bag, the guard stepped back and escorted him out of the shop. Rich was so pissed by the time he was in the main concourse that he wadded up the bag of clothes and walked to the trashcan.

"Yeah, that'll be smart. Throw away our only clothes. I love being seen in these pants that are stained with your food and so many bleach spots that I can't stand it." Rich snarled at Poor. *"Are you pissed because you lost the scent we found, or is it something else? Like the big, bad tiger who made you look bad?"*

"He did no such thing." Rich smelled the air around him and found the scent. *"See, I can still find her."*

The smell was almost gone, but he kept putting his nose in the air and following the little bit that he could get. As soon as he saw the couple he nearly turned back, but the little girl, the little wolf with them, smelled like someone he knew. And he was pretty sure it was the man who'd bloodied him.

Rich couldn't remember all the details, but what he could involved a little girl, a baby, and some pants. He rubbed his head trying to remember. Pain nearly made him whimper, but he had to press on. It wasn't until they entered the toy store that something popped into his head. His enforcer.

"He's the one that made you lose face when you tried to speak to his family. You went to his home because…because…" He tried to help Poor, but there was nothing more there. *"Never mind. You were injured. Let's just focus on that."*

"But I want her, right? There is a reason that I want her and you think it's because I lost something." He felt rather

than heard Poor's answer. *"Yes. I'll snatch her and some of the pack will come back to us if not all."*

He moved to the store and watched them. The male was wolf, but Rich was pretty sure he could get the child without the male knowing it. The female he couldn't get a scent from and was again reminded of something. But it too skittered away. Rich was about to move into the store when the male turned to look at him.

Everything in him froze. His breath, his heart. Rich was pretty sure that even the blood flowing through his veins stopped moving along his limbs in that split second. But then he turned away, dismissed him seemingly. For some reason, or lots of reasons, Rich couldn't tell, that pissed him off.

"You should kill him. Take out that gun you have in your pocket and shoot him right in the head. It will be messy, but it will show everyone that you are something to reckon with." Rich nodded at Poor. *"You should take the female too. The little one. Selling her would give us enough money to buy a one-way ticket out of this stupid town."*

They came out of the store and the little girl had a bag. The older female did as well and the man was holding her hand. Rich followed them out of the mall and into the parking lot. He was nearly on them when the woman suddenly ran back inside the mall. It was now or never.

~~~

Stacy sat on the curb and watched the people come and go. She was waiting for Austin as well as her own alpha. Stacy figured she had only a few more minutes before she was going to be killed. A car pulling up beside her didn't even faze her. But the man who lifted her off the ground did.

"Are you all right?" He seemed to touch her everywhere. "Stacy, are you all right?"

His voice commanded she answer, but she had no strength. She nodded then shook her head and he held her to him. She knew it was Austin and knew it was only a matter of minutes before he snapped her neck.

"I am sorry, alpha. I did not mean to let him be…do you think that he is going to come back?" She wiped at the tears and looked at the bloodied stain near the car they'd come here in. "I only went back to get the gift for the little boy. Something that I thought would make him smile."

"You listen to me, he's going to be fine. Dallas is going to be just fine." Austin let her go and she was engulfed in arms again. This time it was Alexis.

"Are you going to kill me now or may I have a few minutes to say goodbye to the children?" Alexis gave her with a strange look. "I know that I have failed you. It is within your rights as my alpha to do what needs to be done."

"No one is going to kill you. Good Christ, woman, we know that you would never do anything that would let Dallas be hurt. At least you were able to save Luna."

She looked from Austin to the little girl. She was no longer crying, but she was bruised. Her sire had hit her twice when she'd tried to bite him. And he'd dropped the gun when she had. Luna had done more to save her mate than she had.

"He was going to take her as well. He said that he could sell her." Stacy sat down again, her legs no longer strong enough to hold her up. "I believe he is mad. He spoke with someone else, someone that was not here. They…it seemed as if they argued."

Connor was suddenly beside her. He looked at her and then pulled her head to his shoulder. "You did exactly what you needed to do. Now we have the backing of the council. We can take his cowardly ass out."

"I did nothing to save him." Connor pulled her head up and then brushed his fingers over her temple. She flinched at the pain and closed her eyes when he showed her the blood there.

"You were injured badly, Stacy. Yet you still managed to save Luna, call to your alpha, and get close enough to Rich so that we have a scent to go on." He gave her the bag that the ambulance driver handed him. "Put this on your head and hush up. We have the prick now and he's fucked with the wrong family."

Austin came back to where they were and sat on the other side of her. She looked down, subservient. He was still her mate's alpha, no matter that she hadn't pledged to him. He lifted her chin and looked into her eyes.

"The doc said that he needs to look at your head." She started to shake her head. "There are humans here and we have to play nicely. Let him look at it before you heal more. Then I will have Alexis take you back to the house. Holly needs your help. Have you reached for Dallas? Gordon has, as have I, and we're not having any luck."

"I have tried, but he is not responding to me. It is as if he is in a cell as my uncle was. Do you think that he has taken him somewhere like that?" Stacy watched as the men around them walked through what she thought of as evidence.

"That or a cave. If the stone is thick enough and if Dallas were weak enough, then maybe. I think it's a cave. Where else would he be staying if not a hidey hole?" Austin put his arm around her. "We'll get him back, Stacy. Then, when we do, I get to kick his ass first."

The medic wanted to take her to the hospital and have x-rays, but she declined. He had assumed that she was distraught over her husband and had tried to soothe her when she tried to move away from his touch.

"Come on, honey. Let me tape this together at least. That way when that husband of yours is found, you won't have to try and outdo him in battle scars."

She didn't know who called the police. She thought maybe it was someone in the crowd that was milling around them. But because Connor was once on the force, as well as Myles, she was given the okay to leave when the medic said she was good to go. Before she left Myles came to talk to her.

"You're very lucky and brave. If you don't mind, I'd like to ask you a few more questions. Questions that the other police won't…they won't know to ask." She nodded at him. "Did you bite him?"

"No, but Luna did. I think her too young to shift but she had his arm in her mouth tightly." She looked at the little girl. Then pulled her hand out of her pocket. "I have this as well as his scent."

The gun was filled with silver. She wasn't sure why she didn't give it to the police when they asked, but she handed it to the big vampire easily. She watched as he sniffed the barrel. He took it and put it into a baggie he took from his own pocket. Then she handed him the bloodied shirt sleeve she had in her hand when she woke up.

He grinned as he took it. "You're very smart. The police would have put this in a little box and put it away. I'm going to give it to the most powerful noses I can think of."

Myles motioned for Austin and handed him the sleeve. He immediately put it to his nose and then handed it to Connor who did the same. Each man that walked up to them put the blood to their noses and smiled. Stacy almost felt sorry for her sire. He wasn't going to go down quickly. These men were going to kill him.

Holly was waiting for her when she got there. Or at least her mother said she was. She was still in the bathroom throwing up. A lot from the sounds of it. When she staggered out a few minutes later she sat down on the couch and pulled a pillow over her belly.

"So far this pregnancy isn't what I thought it would be." She smiled at her mom when she gave her crackers and tea. "And every time I throw up Phil makes me eat something to replace whatever it was. I think he might be at the top of my hit list right now."

"He loves you and hates that you're sick too." Nancy Force sat in the chair next to the couch and picked up some knitting. "Besides, when you're ill at the beginning of the pregnancy, then you'll have an easier time at the end."

Stacy smiled when Holly stuck her tongue out at her mother. Holly turned and looked at her. "I'm supposed to tell you that Dallas is a big boy and will be fine. But in reality, he's a pain in the ass and will probably beat the crap out of the guy who took him and be waiting for them when they show up. Dallas didn't go down easily."

"He was injured when he was taken."

Holly nodded at her.

"He may be hurt badly and then I will be responsible for that as well."

"I think if he heard you speaking like that he'd be upset with you. Now, Holly wants to work with you trying to remember everything you can." Nancy stood up and took her knitting with her. It was a bright blue something. After kissing her daughter she stood before Stacy. "I've not had the chance to welcome you to the family. I'm very happy that you and Dallas finally made the jump and noticed what all of us have seen for months."

With a kiss to her cheek Nancy Force left the room and closed the door softly behind her.

Holly grinned at Stacy. "My mom is the greatest. She can be a pain, too, but she is the greatest." Holly pulled the laptop that was sitting next to her on the couch. "Now then. Was there a car nearby when you came out of the mall? And, if so, what color and make was it?"

The questions went on for hours. By the time she started slowing down Stacy knew three things. She thought maybe they would be able to find Dallas, that she was giving them more information than they ever would have gotten from anyone else, and that Holly Campbell was the scariest woman she'd ever met.

CHAPTER 17

Dallas moved slowly. He didn't want to move because he knew that he would hurt and he wasn't sure if he was alone. He was tied to something, he couldn't tell what, and he was pretty sure that it was nothing more than simple chain holding him. Attached to what, he couldn't tell. He was too hurt to care at the moment. He moaned when he tried to lift his head up to have a better look.

"So, you're awake now. Has anyone ever told you that you're heavy? It took me nearly two hours to get you in here and nearly another hour to get the chains on you." The man shined a light into his face and Dallas flinched away from it. "Be still so I can see your face. I want to see how much damage I did to you."

"If you would untie me then I'll show you how much it hurts. Better yet, I'll return the favor." Dallas didn't move when the man grew closer. He figured he was going to be hit, but what he didn't expect was what he looked like. "Christ, you're huge."

Okay, in hindsight he should have kept his mouth shut. But he'd been surprised. He'd seen some big wolves before, but none as big as this man. When the flashlight hit him in the ribs for the third time Dallas fell into a black void. His last thought was that he hoped the man didn't eat him.

When he woke the second time—or was it the third?—Dallas was alone. He knew that his jaw was broken and that several ribs were as well, but it was his leg that worried him the most. Looking down at it, he saw the bone sticking out at an odd angle. Dallas called his wolf to shift partly, but he was too weak to manage a shift, even a small one. He knew he would have to shift soon or his leg would heal this way. And then it would have to be broken again to heal correctly.

Dallas looked around his surroundings. He knew it was a cave; thick stone walls were everywhere and he knew he was deep enough in the cave that he couldn't see the opening. Moving slowly Dallas tried to get his bearings, but all he did was make himself sick with pain. He reached for Stacy again.

Nothing. He had felt her once or twice when he'd been riding in the back of the van. Her pain rode him more than his own, but he was happy she wasn't hurt too badly. When Dallas had felt the gun at his head back at the mall and Luna tighten her grip on his arm he'd known almost immediately that it was Rich Sterling.

He'd been buckling Luna in the car when she'd whimpered. He thought he'd hurt her, but when she dug her nails into his arm he was about to turn when the gun touched the back of his head.

"Move and we'll kill you." The laughter sent chills up and down his neck and arms. "Poor wants to know if you'll move enough that he can have a chance at you?"

"Sterling?" The gun pressed harder into his scalp. "You let Luna go and I'll come with you with no problems."

The pain in his head was blinding. Dallas started to turn, but Sterling lunged for the little girl. Dallas moved to intercept him and felt the bullet zip by his cheek, opening it up.

"You'll come with me or, so help me, I'll go into that mall and kill that woman you were with." He hit him again. "Why can't you younger pups leave the humans alone and simply stay within your own kind?"

His first thought had been that Sterling didn't recognize his own daughter and then he realized that, for now, she was safe. Dallas moved slowly, mostly because he was dizzy and, secondly, he wanted Sterling to stay focused on him. But Stacy came out of the mall just as Dallas was going to get into the van and go with him.

She had attacked, he knew that. And he knew that she'd been hurt as well. He'd seen her flying across the parking lot as if she'd been a rag doll. When she'd hit the pavement Dallas had tried to go to her, but he was hit again from behind. This time he couldn't get up from it.

The sounds coming from above him echoed around and behind him. Dallas looked into the darkness and watched a sliver of light coming toward him. He knew it was more than likely a flashlight and he also knew that it wasn't his family. The sounds coming toward him were too heavy and shuffled.

"So, did you eat the townspeople or is there enough for later when you get hungry again?" Dallas knew he was baiting the man, but if he could get him to come closer he might be able to hurt him too. "I heard tell of a blob leaving twenty-nine missing in another town. Was that you?"

Sterling started to come toward him, fury in his stance, but he stopped at the last minute and stood very still. Then he started talking and it took Dallas several seconds to realize he wasn't speaking to him.

"I know, I know, but he's just going to get worse if he thinks he can get away with this. I don't know why I can't just kill him." Silence, and Dallas had a feeling that he was listening to someone. "Okay, but for now only. I don't have the time to hang around here. Are you Austin Force?"

Dallas was startled by the question. He thought his brother was here until he realized that Sterling was asking him and not whoever he was speaking to.

"Yes." Then he grinned. "You thinking about dating me?" The stone hit the wall behind him. Dallas had to catch himself when he started to laugh. He needed the guy closer, not taking pot shots at him.

"No, I do not want to date you. I want that brother of yours too. The one from Texas." Dallas wasn't sure who he meant until Sterling spoke again. "Does your mother have a fetish for cowboys?"

Dallas laughed. He couldn't help it. The man was certifiable. Dallas leaned heavily on the rock behind him, felt his wolf stir a bit, and felt the rope bite into his arms. He wasn't sure what to answer when a sudden flare of light illuminated the room. He looked around as best he could without giving away that he really cared. "You want my brother? Why? I thought I was on your shit list." Dallas saw the injuries now. Stacy had gotten in a few, it seemed. "I took your pack, didn't I?"

"Because that piece of shit thinks he can mate with my daughter." He seemed to be listening to something or someone again. "What's her name? Poor thinks it's a common name like her mother's."

"Her name? It's April. April Force. And she's very happy where she is. I hear tell that they're going to move on soon. Probably to some other state." Dallas didn't want him anywhere near his mate or is brother. "You should probably do your worst to me and forget them."

"No, no, no, no. I want them dead too. They have taken everything from me." Then Sterling put his hand over his ears and started to hum. "I won't listen to you anymore. You aren't real. La, la, la, la."

This went on for perhaps five minutes. Sterling making noises like he was trying to drown someone out then speaking to what Dallas now assumed was the person he called Poor.

"He wants me to kill you now." Dallas didn't move; he was afraid the man would actually do it. "He said that you're no better than your brother and that I should kill you."

"Who wants you to kill me?"

The man seemed to have another conversation then looked right at Dallas. "I'm the other one. Poor, he calls me. I can take him over now, but not for long. Where is the gun?"

Like he'd tell him. Dallas shrugged and then moved his leg. He still didn't have enough strength to shift, but he could get ready. He reached for Austin and felt a very small connection.

"I'm in a cave. Not far from the mall. There should be a gray van with the last three letters seven twenty-one."

"You all right?"

Dallas grinned as he told his brother yes.

"Stacy said she's going to kick your ass when you get back here. She wants to know if she can come and get you or do you think you can help her by killing the bastard and coming home on your own?"

Dallas knew she was scared. He would be if it were him waiting for her to come to him. *"Tell her that I might need her to save me. Tell her...Austin, will you tell her that I love her very much?"*

"Yes. I love you too, you big oaf."

He lost him for several minutes, but Dallas felt better just for having spoken to him. He watched as Sterling paced the cave and tried to reach for Stacy. He was surprised when she answered so clearly.

"I am near to where the van he took you in is parked. Your brother has a fix on the GPS in the van. It is pinging back to them. Also, your cell is on. Are you hurt badly?"

"My leg is broken and healing. I need to shift, but I'm afraid that dumbass here is going to kill me." He paused long enough to try and see if she was close to him. *"You aren't alone, are you?"*

"Yes. I can move faster without others with me." He felt her humor. *"Your brother believes I am in the bathroom being ill. He does not know that your other brother has been telling me where to go by cell phone. Connor is quite good at this."*

And when Dallas got back home he was going to hug him. Then beat the shit out of him for allowing his mate to go out on her own. She was too precious to allow anything to—

"Would you like to know something else?"

He told her he would.

"Your sister has invited me to—" He was terrified when she suddenly stopped. Before he could beg her to go back home and wait for him, she spoke again. *"I have found the van. It is in a parking space at a state park. If it is here then you must be close."*

"I'm going to kill you. Now, as a matter of fact. Richard has completely lost his mind and I've decided that you are a liability rather than a help." Sterling, or whoever he was, came toward him as he spoke. "I hope you have your house in order. It would be a shame for it not to be."

"And you think I'm going to lay here and let you?" He tried to reach for Stacy, suddenly needing her to hurry up. "Bring it on, nutcase. I'm ready for whatever you think you can dish out."

~~~

Stacy shifted again and moved up the mountain. She had been here before and knew the area. She had even slept in one of the caves because she had thought she was being followed. About halfway up she ran into three wolves trying to bring down a deer.

They were wild and hungry. She tried to skirt around them, but one of them saw her and snarled. Stacy growled low and raised her hackles. She was much bigger than them and had a great deal more experience fighting her kind. She watched as they began to circle her. That's when she saw the opening of the cave and the trash sitting outside of it.

"Okay, big guys, I do not want your meat. I have more important things to do than play with you." One of them crouched down and was starting to lunge when something flashed between them.

"Go now. I have this."

She looked at Myles.

"I said to go. I want to show them what a vampire can do when he's pissed."

Stacy wanted to make sure Myles was all right, but she needed to get to Dallas. Racing up the hill without a backward glance she moved to the mouth of the cave and started in. She nearly leapt with joy when she smelled her mate.

"I am coming." She didn't know what to expect when Dallas did not answer, but hurried to climb down into the belly of the cave. What she saw when she got there would be a memory that she'd never forget.

Dallas lay on the ground, his leg broken. She could see the bone sticking up from his calf as if it were a stick. She moved slowly around the cave, not making a sound, hoping to see what she was up against.

"You've been a pain in my ass since I was born."

She stopped suddenly and looked at the man standing over Dallas.

"I could have been great if not for you."

"You didn't even know me when you were a kid. How the hell is it possible that I have been a pain in *your* ass? You're a moron, did you know that?" Dallas caught her eye and looked to his left. That's when she saw the long sword that was in her sire's hand. "Why don't you come on around to the right and take me out? You too chicken to fight like a real man?"

She nearly did not catch what he was trying to tell her. She'd been so focused on the blade that was pointed into Dallas' chest that she didn't see that the fire was just to the right and if she attacked from there, she could use the pit to her advantage. Circling to her left, she kept to the darkness.

"You made me fat."

That startled her. How did one make another fat?

"And you took all my money."

"I did take your money. Yeah, can't deny that."

She was nearly to her sire when he turned to look right at her. "What have we here?"

She leapt at him just as he brought the sword up. She didn't have time to catch herself so when the blade pierced her chest she opened her jaws wide and bit down just as they both tumbled to the ground.

Blood filled her mouth, though she was not sure it if were his or hers. She shook her head as she heard Dallas scream out her name. This ended now and she was not going to let him go until she knew he was dead.

Blackness tried to take away her sight, but she fought it. Even as her sire struggled less and less, she did not let go. Dallas was saying her name, telling her that she'd killed him, when she felt his hand along her fur.

"Let him go, love, so that I can take you to be healed."

She heard the words, but didn't understand them.

"Come on, baby. I have to get you help. I won't allow you to die."

She shifted. As soon as she did he pulled her into his arms. "You are safe now." He nodded and she wiped away the tear. "I love you."

"I love you too." She was starting to fade out. When she opened her eyes again he was right there. Smiling softly, she touched his face, or she tried to. "I have given you everything. My sire did not own the land that was his pack." She moved his hand when he put it over her mouth. Blood stained his fingers. "You will be happy now. Run a pack like it should be."

"Don't talk. Help is coming. The doc, Clint, is coming, and he said to keep you quiet."

Stacy wasn't stupid. She was dying. Coughing slightly, she felt warmth spill from her mouth. She looked down at the sword still sticking in her chest.

There was a moment of complete clarity and she looked up to tell Dallas what she thought. He was blurred and she wanted to bring his mouth to hers, but she couldn't manage her hands. Shifting slightly, she moaned. So much pain, yet she wasn't sure she was feeling it all. Closing her eyes against a sudden light she heard Dallas sob, but she couldn't help him. Soon he'd be with his family and forget her after a time.

"No you don't."

She moved away from the light and then she cried out. Pain was everywhere, then nothing.

CHAPTER 18

Dallas moved into the yard to watch the workers. He still wasn't steady on his injured leg. Hell, everyone knew it wasn't going to get any better. The rows of neat little houses were coming along nicely and he was glad to see the first houses were being moved into as he watched.

"There will be more built in the coming months. Soon we'll have to move onto the property that Stacy gave you." Dallas looked at Austin and Connor as they sat next to him. Connor continued as he pulled a bottle of beer from the cooler. "I wanted to talk to you about the property on the southeast corner. I'd like to buy it from you."

He glanced at his brother and declined the beer. "Take it. It's yours. I've no use for something so far from home."

He noticed the glance between the two of them, but ignored it. He'd been seeing the same look for days now and didn't really care for it. He was depressed, damn it, and he wished they'd leave him the fuck alone. He nearly groaned when he saw CJ coming toward them.

"I have a project for you, Dallas. I was wondering if you could go to the other end of my old place and see what's going on with the woman who's living there. She and a couple of the other workers said they heard a lot of noises last night and want someone to check it out."

"It wasn't me. And if you want someone to check it out, send Connor. You know that I can't walk well yet." He didn't even bother looking this time; he knew what they were thinking. "Don't you guys have someone else to bother?"

"Not at the moment." Austin pulled CJ into his lap and held her. "You should see what Lee has been up to. He can climb that bookshelf like it's a step ladder."

He didn't want to move from where he was. And Dallas just wanted them to leave him to himself. He looked at his watch then up at the sunlight streaming through the trees. Soon. Soon now and he'd be with her.

He did groan when Phil and Myles came to sit with him. Didn't these people have anything better to do? Dallas looked at his watch again. Still plenty of time to get home yet.

"She called."

He looked sharply at CJ.

"About ten minutes ago. She said that she was going to be home early and she would come over here and see me when she got off. I would imagine that she's about here."

Dallas stood up and reached for his crutches. They were in Phil's hand and he didn't look as if he was going to hand them over. Dallas didn't have time for this shit and put out his hand for them.

"Come and get them." Phil stood up and took several steps back. "You know you want them, so come and get them from me."

"I can't. You know that too." He reached again for them only to have Phil take another step back. "Give them to me, Phil. I want to go home."

"Then get them." He looked over at Stacy, the love of his life and wondered how long she'd been standing there. "Go and get them and I will take you home with me. Otherwise I will leave you here."

"I can't." He heard the others leave and was glad for it. If he was going to grovel then he'd rather do so without an audience. "You heard what the doctor said. I'm deformed."

"No, he did not. He said you would have a limp. That is not the same. You have been nursing this wound for several weeks now. It is time that you get over yourself and walk. No one cares that you will limp."

He did. But instead of moving toward her as she wanted, he sat back down. "Then I'll just stay here."

"And our child? What of him?"

He looked at her quickly then away.

"You do not believe me? What shall I tell him of his father when he asks where you might be. Should I tell him he mopes beneath a maple tree as if it is his business?"

"I would know if you were with child. I haven't slept with you for…" He glanced at her then at the houses again. "You know how long it's been."

"Yes. Since I was stabbed saving your life. A life you have decided to waste by not doing what the doctor said."

He sat back, not wanting to get into this argument again. "Are you going to let me take your picture so that I may show our child what his father looks like?"

"And what of you?" He turned to her viciously. "Why don't you show me your scar? The one you hid away in the darkness of the night. Do you think your wounds are any less horrific than mine?"

She walked to him and when she was within two feet of him she began unbuttoning her blouse. When she dropped it on the ground beside him, he noticed that she was wearing another shirt under it. Before he could comment on that, she started talking.

"I was not hiding the wound, but my belly." The second shirt slipped over her head and she put her hands on her middle. "I had hoped we would touch him, speak to him in our bed, but you have not been there for many weeks. And now look at me. Large and without a mate to share it with."

She was too. He wanted to reach out and run his hands over her swollen belly, but was afraid that he'd somehow ruin it. He watched her as she rubbed it, rubbed their child. He wanted to look away, but Dallas simply couldn't make himself. "You could have told me." He did reach out then and she pressed his hand to her. Movement, very slight, brushed against this hand.

"I could have. But I had hoped you would come to me." She took a step back from him. "Dallas, you must come to our home. I'm lonely there without you."

He looked down at his leg. It had healed too much for them to do much more than break it and hope it would set on its own. It had, but not properly. Clint Burris, the pack doctor, told him he'd been lucky. Lucky? Not from where he was sitting.

"I can't walk without falling on my ass. And even though no one has said anything I can see that they're laughing at me." He watched as a little girl came across the way toward them. Stacy put her shirt back on and they both waited for Luna.

"Hello. I was wondering when you were going to come to my new house." She crawled up into his lap and settled herself in his arms. "It's a very lovely house. My mom keeps turning on the water. And she makes me take a bath every day."

"You should. It will keep you healthy." He wrapped his arm around her. "I will come to see your new house when they get the cart I need to walk."

"You're just being a poop head. My mom said that you could walk if you wanted to. She said you were being a poop head because there are a lot of people out there that have no legs and you act like you have it worse." Luna sat up and looked at him. "Are you a poop head?"

"No, I am not." He tried to take the heat out of his voice, but she stiffened in his arms anyway. "I'm just a man who was hurt, that's all. It'll take time for it to heal and it's not been nearly long enough."

She turned in his arms and then looked at Stacy. "You think he's a poop head, Stacy? I think he is. Nobody can sit around all day and not want to play. You never play."

Dallas looked at Stacy and thought about how much he missed playing with her. It had been weeks and he was missing her body next to his. He moved Luna off him and pulled the pillow over his lap. He wasn't going to explain how hard he was to a six-year-old.

Stacy moaned softly, but he heard it. Luna was talking a little more, but he was beyond hearing her. His mate was aroused. As soon as Luna moved off to play with her new friends Stacy stood up.

"Come here to me. I want you."

She shook her head at him.

"Please, Stacy, I need you, want you."

She moved back from where she'd come from. "Then come home. I will be naked in our bed awaiting you. If you do not come to me tonight, I will leave you, Dallas. I do not have the time to raise a second child as big as you are. Come to me tonight or we go our separate ways."

"And our child?" He was sick to death of people trying to get him to do things by blackmailing him. And he'd expected more from her. "What will you tell our child?"

"That his father gave up on himself."

Dallas watched her walk into the woods. She would come back anytime now and he knew it. After several minutes he shouted for her and she didn't come back. It wasn't until it started to rain that he realized she wasn't coming back for him. The movement of the chair next to him had him look over at his mom.

"She's stubborn, isn't she?"

Dallas nodded, too pissed to speak to his own mother.

"I would imagine she'll need to be if she has to raise that child on her own."

"She wouldn't have to if she came back here." He looked over at his mom just realizing what she'd said. "You knew about this? You knew she was going to leave me?"

That damned wooden spoon hit him square in the forehead. And he reached up to snatch it from her when she hit him again. He frowned at her and counted to ten. Then twenty. He was nearly to fifty when she spoke to him.

"Are you just going to let her go? Are you going to sit here on your lazy, sorry ass and let her walk out of your life? With your child?" She put the stick on the table between them. "And here I thought of all my children, you would get it the most."

"Get what?" He glanced at the spoon wondering if he could get if before she did. "And in case you didn't get it, she's leaving me."

His mom stood up and looked down at him. "I wouldn't have ever thought it possible. A son of mine that is no better...no better than the monster she killed to save you."

"I'm nothing like her sire. He murdered for money. He took and took until there was nothing left to take, then he took more."

"And you are so different how? Did you take her love? Did you take her heart?" She picked up the spoon. "Yes, you did. At least he had reasons for leaving his daughter. You've simply given up."

"I've not given up anything." He rubbed his hand over his aching heart. "She and everyone else wants more from me than I have to give."

"Do they, Dallas?" She looked at the forest then spoke softly. "Did you ever know that your father lost his thumb?"

"No. He had all his fingers, Mom. What are you talking about?" Then he remembered his dad not being able to do some things the way he'd done them. He'd figured out different ways to— "Yeah. Yeah, I remember. He lost it when he was still a pup."

"Yes. But you think it stopped him from doing things he wanted? Do you ever remember seeing him act like he wasn't a whole man?" She looked at him with a tear in her eye. "Did you ever once hear him say he couldn't because he wasn't all there?" She walked back to the house. She closed the door behind her. His crutches were still far away and the misty rain had turned to a downpour.

"Mother fuck," he shouted to the sky. "What the fuck am I supposed to do now? Crawl to you?"

He glared at the spoon and thought about how many times over the years he'd wanted to burn the sucker. Chop it up into little pieces and toss them in the trash can. He reached out and picked it up.

She only hit them with it when she was trying to make a point. He realized that long before now. It didn't make it any less irritating, but he didn't have to like it. Dallas looked at the forest then at the house. Both the women in his life were set to piss him off.

His dad had been a great man. He'd been a wonderful father. But he'd been hurt. Dallas leaned back in his chair and thought about his dad. When he'd been wolf, he'd been unable to run like the others; his lack of thumb had hindered him. It didn't stop him, but it did slow him a little. But there was never a time when his father said "I can't." Never in all Dallas' young life had those words ever crossed his lips.

Dallas stood up and held the spoon in his hand as he held onto the chair. He'd not been putting weight on his leg like he'd been told because…well, he hadn't. He looked at the crutches and realized that he would need them if only to get started. He needed them to get around for now.

Moving slowly he made his way to them when suddenly, there was a shadow over them. He looked up to see his brother Connor. He waited for him to start on him and didn't say a word.

"You want me to follow you for a bit? It might be a little rough at first." Connor handed him the one crutch and laid the other on the chair. "Let's start with this one and work our way down."

Dallas nodded, moved beyond words. His brother wasn't going to make fun of him or try to bully him into anything. Dallas moved slowly forward and nearly fell over. Austin was there to catch him.

"Come on, buddy. We can do this." He was leaning heavily on Austin, waiting for the pain to subside. "Take one little step at first. If you lean on me, I'll catch you. Come on."

He took a smaller step and felt the sweat start to run down his back. Pain shot up his leg and into his hip. And if his steps got any smaller, he'd be going backwards. He looked at Austin, ready to give up.

"You want to play ball with your son? With both our sons?" Dallas nodded at Austin's question. "Then I suggest that you get your ass in gear."

He took three more steps when he felt a hand at his back. Turning so as not to fall, he looked at his brother Gordon. The smile on his face was radiant.

"You didn't think we'd let you do this on your own, did you?" Gordon held onto his belt at the back of his pants. "Alexis said if you make it halfway there, she'll bake you her famous cake. Frankly, I hope you don't. I love that cake and don't want to share."

"I don't even like cake and I love it. Hello, big guy. You ready for the last mile?"

Dallas looked at Phil and Myles. They were both standing in front of him with their arms crossed over their chests.

"Don't just stand there gaping like a fish, get your ass in gear."

Dallas couldn't move. He held onto his crutch and looked at the men in his life. Family. They were all his family. He cleared his throat three times before he could speak.

"I was thinking about Dad just now. And how he never said 'I can't.' I've been such a wuss the past three months."

Austin nodded.

"I just didn't want to...I wanted to be the big, bad enforcer, and now...I'm not anything to anyone now." He raised his hand when they looked ready to argue. "I've changed my mind. I am someone. I'm going to be a dad. And I'm going to be the best dad I can be."

"Sure you will. If you get to your house." Austin helped him move, as did the rest. They were halfway to the house, about a mile, when he couldn't go any further. They helped him sit against a tree while Phil stepped away to make a call.

"I can take it from here, boys. Provided you can help me get him in the car."

He looked up to see Stacy.

"I can get him out, but getting him in might pose a problem for me."

In ten minutes he was buckled into the new SUV she'd gotten them. He'd wondered why she needed something so big, and now he understood. He realized how much he'd missed staying at the pack house to heal. They were driving along when he reached out to take her hand.

"I'm so sorry."

She nodded, tears running down her face.

"I love you, Stacy. I'm so sorry for all I've put you through."

"You can make it up to me if you let me take you to bed when we get home. I know you'll want to rest, but I simply want to hold on to you."

He nodded and laid his head against the head rest.

He needed to hold her too, he realized. He was going to make this work if it was the last thing he did. When they pulled up in front of the house he swallowed his pride and asked her to help him. Leaning on her felt good. Needing her felt amazing.

CHAPTER 19

Four months later

"Pack law states that in order for you to be an alpha in your own right, you have to…"

Stacy growled at the man in front of her. Nigel Briggs had been a pain in her butt since she'd filed a claim to the property that her mother had left her. Briggs took two steps back. She was nearly nine months pregnant, hot, and tired. And this idiot was quoting bylaws at her. As if she had not read them a thousand times over the past several months.

"If you say to me once more that I have to be claimed by my sire, I shall hurt you." She took a deep breath. "I have told you many times that he is deceased. My mother is deceased. They are all dead."

"But you have no claim that says you are who you say you are." He opened the book again then closed it quickly when she growled again. "If you had but a birth certificate, then I could simply file what needed to be filed. As it stands now, there is—"

"Sorry we're late."

She looked up at Phil and her uncle.

"We had to find a few things before we could make this meeting."

Dallas walked into the room at that moment and she wanted to scream. He leaned down, kissed her forehead, and sat next to her. He'd been in a meeting when this idiot showed up forty-five minutes late for their meeting and had not been able to join them. She wanted to take a nap and her back was hurting her again.

"Sir. As I have said to your mate, without proper identification, or someone that can verify that she is who she claims she is, then I'm sorry, but the council has no choice but to claim the property as its own." He started to stand and sat down when Dallas stood as well. "There are people who know where I am."

Phil laughed and she glared. "I'm sure we can finish this without resorting to whatever mayhem is running through her mate's mind right now. You said she needed proof. Would her birth certificate be enough?"

She felt his touch seconds before he spoke to her. *"You want this property then I suggest you let me do the talking."*

Stacy glared at Phil. She knew that since Myles had given her his blood, she had a connection to his maker as well. She wasn't thrilled by it, but simply tried to forget about it. She also knew there was no birth certificate.

"I was about to have him for dinner. If you let me, I'll let you have first taste." She nearly choked on her glass of water when Phil licked his lips at her. The councilman didn't seem to think it was funny.

"I thought you said that no record of…" The man seemed to understand that he was in a house full of people that could and would eat him if this went on much longer. "Let me have a look at this."

In the forty hours he looked it over Stacy tried to think of anything. Of course it wasn't really that long, it just seemed that way. She shifted on her chair again and wondered if she could have someone find her a heating pad. Phil suddenly looked up at her.

"How long, Stacy?"

She looked at him, frowning.

"How long have you been in labor?"

"I am not in labor." She looked at Dallas, panicky. "I am not in labor. I have five days to go."

He grinned. "I don't think our son cares about those five days. I felt your pain an hour ago. I had hoped that you'd be finished with this gentleman and we could go to the clinic. I've called Clint and told him we were coming."

Stacy looked at Briggs. "Do you know how to deliver a baby? If not then I would suggest that you sign that stupid paper and let me go have my child."

He snatched the pen that Phil was handing him and scribbled his name over the document. She had a sudden thought as to if he was hitting the correct line when a sudden ripping pain took her breath away.

"Okay then" Phil put the document into the file and looked at them all. "Dallas, pick up your lovely mate. Myles, call the troops. I'll get them to the hospital right—"

"No," Dallas said loudly. "No, you're not taking them that way. You can't make her sick when she's in labor. We'll drive. A car. My car."

Phil laughed. "I was going to say the car. I wouldn't do that to her. You maybe, but not her."

They had her loaded in the back of the SUV in seconds and Phil was driving them to the hospital. She was trying to get a grip on her pain and breathing when she felt her water break. Suddenly, things seemed to slow. She felt calm, almost like she was prepared for anything.

She was going to be a mother and it was going to happen now. Stacy looked at Dallas, who looked terrified. Stacy put her hand to his cheek. Things were going to be fine. They were going to be fine.

There seemed to be too many people waiting for them. As soon as they stopped, all the doors flew open and she was lifted from Dallas' arms. The ride inside was on a gurney and she looked around the emergency room. There seemed to be every person they knew and then some.

She had never felt so loved in her entire life. Smiling, she was whisked to the second floor and labor and delivery. Nancy Wolf was already there waiting.

"That nice man Myles brought me. He said it usually made people sick to be taken that fast, but he said Phil showed him how to do it without causing problems." Stacy would have laughed at the expression on Dallas' face, but another pain took her. "Oh my, dear, you must hurry."

~~~

Dallas held her hand. He was exhausted and he was sure she was too. They'd been at this for nearly three hours and things were not progressing like they had been told it would in those labor classes. In fact, they made it seem so easy. He looked at the monitor when it starting beeping again.

Clint came in smiling and Dallas decided that when this was over, he was going to have Phil drain him. There was something purely sadistic about the man. Who left a woman in labor for this long and smiled?

"Okay, Stacy. Let's see how you're coming along." He moved to the foot of the bed. When he hummed for the second time, then a third, Dallas was trying to figure out what it would cost for a hired gun. Maybe he could get a discount from Holly.

"Well?" He looked around the room when he realized he was being stared at. *Okay*, he thought, *take a deep breath and try again.* "Well? Is she progressing?"

"Yep."

What kind of doctor said "yep" like a ten-year-old anyway?

"I think we should move this along now. I'd say you're ripe for the picking, Stacy. I'm ready if you are."

She nodded. Dallas didn't. Now? They were ready now? Before he could voice his concerns the room was filled with people and he was being placed at the head of the table near Stacy's head. He nearly said stop when Clint told her to push when she felt the next contraction.

"I think—" Stacy howled and the hair on his arms rose up. Suddenly she had a grip on his arms that made him see stars. They were having a baby.

They'd not wanted to know the sex. He and Stacy had decided that when the baby came they'd be happy. Healthy was really all they wanted and when he was born, they'd name him then. Dallas secretly wanted to name him after his father, but didn't want to push the issue. Not yet at any rate. His son, the doctor said, was crowning.

Four pushes later it was finished. When Clint put the baby onto her chest Stacy cried. It was all Dallas could do not to join her. He looked down at his precious bundle and touched the tiny little fingers. They were as soft as they looked.

"You should go and tell your family."

He nodded, but didn't move.

"Dallas, you made a promise to them. If they did not join us in this room then you would come tell them as soon as it was over."

He moved to the door, glancing back every second or so. He couldn't have wiped the grin off his face if he'd had a gun to his head. Entering the waiting room, he chuckled. It looked like the entire pack, both his and Austin's, were there.

His mom stepped forward.

"She's all right. And so is my daughter. All nine pounds and eleven ounces of her."

The room erupted in congratulations and well wishes. His mom hugged him to her and laughed. "I knew it was going to be a girl. You've your work cut out for you."

Dallas kissed her on the cheek. "We had a girl's name picked out. Just in case I was wrong this time. The only one we agreed on. Her name is Nancy Janelle Force." His mom hugged him tighter. "I love you, Mom."

"And I love you, son. I can't believe..." She looked around the room. "We've so much here. So much that I can't..."

"I love you, Mom." He wanted to go back to Stacy, but knew that his mom needed him more than ever. "When I grow up, I want to be just like you."

She laughed as he'd hoped she would. He held her while his brothers patted him on the back and congratulated him. Even Phil, with his own baby cradled in his arms, seemed to understand that he was a part of something huge here. He nodded as if to say he really did understand.

After his family held little Nancy and ooed and ahhed over her they went home. Dallas sat on the chair next to Stacy's bed and watched his daughter breathe. It was by far the most exciting thing he'd ever seen. When Stacy yawned again he turned off the light and held her.

"I want to have several more children, Dallas. Would that be all right with you?"

He nodded, closing his eyes.

"And I want us to let my uncle come and stay with us if you do not mind."

He didn't. He had grown very fond of the older wolf. He grinned when he thought of his face when Dallas told him to come to live with them. He was a man who didn't like change. Dallas decided that he'd ask him to be his council. That might make it easier.

"Harvey said that he would help me. I think that I'll ask him about it tomorrow. You and I have a nice pack to run." Not all that large, but it was getting bigger daily. Nearly all of Stacy's sire's pack had asked to be with her. It seemed that Stacy had been helping them for years.

"Dallas, do you think it bad if we simply held her while she slept?" He got up and went to the little bassinet. Picking her up, she snored slightly and he laughed. Handing her to Stacy, she smiled and pulled her to her breast. "We have a beautiful little girl."

"Yes. And her mother is beautiful as well." He reached into the little drawer beside the bed, pulled out the small package, and handed it to her. "I love you and wanted you to have something for making me the happiest man in the world. I know that sounds sappy, but I am."

She handed him Nancy and opened the box. He held his breath as she fumbled with the tape. When she tried to peel away the wrapping without tearing it he nearly told her to simply tear it off. But he didn't. He smiled when she finally opened the box.

It was a bracelet. One he'd had made for her. She took it out and held it to her cheek. He leaned over their daughter and kissed her.

He'd talked with his brother on the design. It had taken them nearly a month to decide on it and he'd never been so pleased with anything like he was with this. Connor promised him that he'd never use the design again for anything.

The wolves chasing one another were made of white gold and encircled her wrist perfectly. The chain that held them together was made of copper. He'd had his brother add a few stones, things he'd found for her when they'd been walking the property. Nothing precious, but things they'd both loved. Then there was the beautiful emerald that was on the clasp. It had been his father's signet ring from college. His mom had given him the broken ring and told him to use the gold. They had. Each wolf had a little of the white gold in them.

"I have something for you as well." She had him hand her the bag his mom had brought to the hospital. "It has been in my purse for nearly a month. I wanted to surprise you with it."

He took the small box and didn't know what to say. He'd never been very good at receiving gifts. He was more of a giver. He tore the paper off much to her delight and smiled before he opened it.

"Oh ,Stacy." The framed picture lay nestled in a bed of tissue paper. He didn't even try to lift it out, terrified that he'd break it. It wasn't so much the frame, but the picture itself. "It's all of us."

The picture was perhaps forty years old. In it were his mom and dad and his brothers. They were standing in front of the house he'd grown up in. He and Austin were about ten and the others just a few years younger. His parents were looking at each other as if they were so deeply in love. He and his brothers were standing shoulder to shoulder with their arms around each other and the most mysterious smiles on their faces. As if they knew as soon as the picture was taken they were going to get into trouble for something big.

"Your mother said you broke your arm that afternoon. She said that Austin had tossed you from a tree to see if you could fly." She looked at the picture with him. "Why would someone do that to his own brother?"

"We had a bet. I was the flyer first because I won. Austin was a little pissy because he wanted to fly first. It never occurred to us that we couldn't. My parents made us believe we could do anything." He ran his finger over his father's face, only now realizing how much he and Austin looked like him. "Dad said that the next time we decided to see if we could do something that involved anything sharp or high off the ground we had to make sure he was there to help us."

"I am sure that he would have talked you out of such foolishness. To think you thought you could fly." She took Nancy from him and he laughed. "You will not teach our daughter such tricks. She will remain a lady."

Dallas only nodded. With as many pack and cousins she had already he doubted his daughter would be anything less than a boy at heart. He smiled when he thought of Holly helping her be all the boy she could be. Snuggling into his mate's body, he smiled again. "You can try, love, but I'm pretty sure when she gets old enough, neither of us will be able to stop her."

Stacy snorted.

"Our best bet is to try and be there when she falls."

"I suppose it will be good for her when she starts to date. Knowing how to protect herself from other males." Stacy turned off the light.

Dallas laid there thinking of all the things he was going to do to the first male that even looked his daughter's way. And he smiled the entire time. His daughter was not going to date until she was at least thirty and then only if he was there with her. No one was going to hurt one of his.

ABOUT THE AUTHOR

I woke up one morning and decided to give play time to the people in my head who were keeping me awake. Little did I know that they would be so relentless and want their time right now! I wrote for the pure joy of it and to entertain my family and friends. But mostly it was to get more than an hour of sleep without a story playing out. Of course, the more I write, the more they want. So…well, as a result of sleepless days (I work through the night as a gun toting grandma – nope not a vigilantly but an armed security guard) I have lots of stories written.

Hello! My name is Kathi Barton and I'm an author. I have been married to my very best friend Sonny for at times seems several lifetimes – in a good way, honey. And together we have three wonderful children and then the ones we brought into the world - Paul and Dale Barton, Jason and Wendy Barton and Danielle and Ben Conklin. They have given us seven of the greatest treasures on Earth. They don't live at home seven days a week! No, seriously, seven grandchildren – Gavin, Spring, Ben, Trinity, Sarah, Kelly and Kian.

Follow Kathi on her blog:
http://kathisbartonauthor.blogspot.com/

www.ingramcontent.com/pod-product-compliance
Lightning Source LLC
Chambersburg PA
CBHW030316180626
46810CB00003B/1113